LIKE *birds* IN THE WILDERNESS

LIKE *birds* IN THE WILDERNESS

Agnes Owens

Fourth Estate · London

First published in Great Britain by
Fourth Estate Limited
113 Westbourne Grove
London W2 4UP

British Library Cataloguing in Publication Data

Owens, Agnes
Like birds in the wilderness.
1. Title
823'.914[F] PR6065.W47/

ISBN 0-947795-51-0

Typeset in Bodoni by Rapidset, London
Printed and bound in Great Britain by The Bath Press, Avon

Also by Agnes Owens:

Gentlemen of the West

CHAPTER 1

All day I had tramped the streets of this strange city in a fruitless search for work, head bent against the wind and lugging my shabby hold-all. Already my money was spent on scrappy meals and fags. The only thing I possessed to the good was an address for a lodging house obtained from the local Department of Health and Social Security, but since they were unwilling to advance me the rent I had slight hope of being accepted. All the same, I decided to try it. I was cold, tired and hungry. One night's kip was my present notion of paradise. I stopped a guy to ask the way. He told me to cut along Barrack Road, first on the left, until I reached Hawkers' Lane, second on my right, then to carry on until I reached the cenotaph. He was still mouthing directions when I left him. Eventually I reached my goal, one of a row of faded Georgian terraces.

A dour-faced youth answered the door. I explained that the broo had sent me.

'Broo?' he questioned.

'Labour exchange, then. They said ye took in ludgers.'

He jerked his head backwards to convey that I should follow him down a long lobby into a big kitchen that smelled of onions.

'Wait here till I fetch ma Da,' he said.

I sat at a big table covered with an oilcloth and faced a pot on the cooker. It was boiling over. I felt I should turn off the gas, or at the least turn it down, but I was afraid that I might appear forward. I became agitated with the problem and had decided to creep away from it all when the youth returned with a stockily built man who said straight away, 'It's sixteen pounds a week for yer digs. Danny here will show ye the layout and the rules. Take note that we don't put up wi' drinkin' in the rooms, women in the rooms, or ony other kind o' activity, apart frae sleepin'.'

'Sixteen pounds a week,' I said thoughtfully.

'We're wan o' the cheapest places aboot here, but if ye don't fancy it . . .'

Quickly I said, 'That's fine, but can ye wait until Friday for the money, since I've jist newly started work?'

There was no point in telling him otherwise. I sensed he wasn't the type to take chances with an unemployed brickie.

'So long as ye're workin', ye can pay a tenner a week extra until ye're clear.' He passed me over to Danny who gave me another jerk of the head. I followed him out of the kitchen. The pot was still boiling over.

Some time later I returned to the kitchen, dampened by the sight of the sleeping quarters, which I was to share with another two guys. This was a big square room, furnished with three narrow beds pressed against the walls and a huge dark wardrobe – reminiscent of the kind seen in old creepy silent films, wherein some mad creature lurks. The walls themselves were emulsioned a brownish yellow that may or may not have been the colour of the original paint. The floor was stained the same dark colour as the wardrobe, and the carpet in the centre of all this was threadbare. My brain was further dulled by Danny's tight-lipped references to the required code of conduct expected from boarders, which apart from no drinking and no women – as ordered by his Da – included no visitors of any kind, no eating, no pets and no music in the room. I wondered if he was all there in the head. An elderly man, possibly in his late fifties, sat at a table engrossed in a newspaper spread out in front of him. He said, 'Good evening,' and returned his attention to the paper. I asked him at what time the dinner was served.

'When everybody's in,' he said with a furtive look towards Danny who was stirring the same pot that had boiled over.

'When will that be?'

He leaned over and whispered, 'Ye canny tell exactly, but onyway,' he added winking, 'it helps if ye're hungry.'

He looked back at his newspaper and studied the sports page through a pair of thin gold-framed spectacles, similar to the type Woolworth's used to sell. I was reminded of a model house lodger who takes pains to look tidy against the odds.

Two guys entered and scraped back the chairs in a way that put my teeth on edge. They began to strum their fingers on the table, fixing their eyes in a direction opposite mine. They wore the building site gear. You could tell this from the clay marks.

'Whit's the poison?' one of them asked the old man. He was red-haired and maybe about my age, which is twenty-three.

'Stovies.'

Both guys howled simultaneously. 'Stovies!'

Danny looked up from the cooker. 'Don't gimmy ony lip,' he shouted as he shook a wooden spoon. The guys shrugged, and one began to strum again. The red-haired guy grabbed at the elderly guy's paper saying, 'Gie us a read at that paper, Dad,' and tearing it in the process.

'Just when I wis studyin' form,' said the old man.

'Ye likely stole it onyway,' said red-hair throwing the paper back to the elderly guy. He finally acknowledged my presence by saying, 'Keep an eye on auld Dad here. He's a con-man by trade and a tea leaf on the side.'

'I've nothin' tae steal.' I laughed and drew my chair close to the table, glad to be included in the company.

The seats filled up gradually. Ten men sat at the table, all dressed in the working gear, except Dad. I wore the working gear too, since it's all I had. Danny hurled over a trolley full of steaming plates. He skimmed each one round to us as though he was playing quoits. I looked close at my heap of brown mashed potatoes.

'Where's the meat?' I asked.

'In wi' the tatties. Have ye no' had stovies afore?'

I shovelled down the stodge quickly in order to calm my rumbling stomach.

'Is it always as good as this?' I asked Dad when I had scraped my plate clean.

'Not always,' he answered, searching my face perhaps for a trace of irony. He cut through his pile of potatoes as though he was dealing with steak. He appeared to be a delicate eater. I leaned back and tried to force out a belch as a mark of appreciation, but didn't quite make it. I asked if there was any pudding to follow. 'Only breid and cheese,' said one of the lodgers in a mournful way. I nodded as though I wasn't bothering. Afterwards we all drifted into another big room containing some tattered couches and chairs and, surprisingly, a colour television – all, that is, except Dad who had gone out the front door. Immediately the seats were occupied and I was left standing. 'Sit here,' said the red-haired guy, squeezing up to offer me some space beside him on the couch. I perched myself on the edge, forced to lean forward and face the television as if I was absorbed in it, though I couldn't hear a word for the hum of voices around me.

'Pipe doon everybody,' someone called, 'I want tae listen tae the telly and so does that new fella.'

'I'm no' botherin',' I said. Everyone was staring at me. I closed my eyes and pressed myself back against the couch.

'Well ye can see he's tired,' said the same guy. 'Gie him a bit o' peace and quiet.'

'How can he be tired,' someone else said. 'He's no' been here long enough to get tired.'

When an argument arose among them about whether I should be tired or not I stood up and turned off the television.

'Is that whit ye want?' I asked.

Everyone looked away and began to talk amongst themselves except the guy who had wanted to watch the television. He started to protest and was told to belt up once and for all. The red-haired guy handed me a fag. I squeezed back into my space and we began to talk. I explained that I had come up here to look for work.

'But that's great,' he said. 'We're needin' a brickie to make up the squad on oor site. Ye can start first thing in the mornin'.'

'Are ye sure?'

'Sure, I'm sure.' He added, 'By the way whit's yer name? Mine's Jimmy.'

'Mac,' I said as we shook hands.

I then suggested that he lend me a fiver so I could buy him a drink, saying I would pay it back plus two pounds extra for his trouble when I got a wage.

He pondered this for a minute, then said with a grin on his freckled face, 'I think that's a great idea.'

The pub, named The Potted Head, was heavy with smoke and loud with the high-pitched northern twang. We sat with our pints at a table for two, well back from the bar and facing the entrance. Jimmy did most of the talking. His subject was mainly women. His attention was continually distracted by their arrival into the pub. I suspected he had deliberately picked the table for the view.

'Whit aboot yersel'?' he said. 'Hiv ye got a bit o' stuff?'

'Naw – er – that is, no' at the moment. I mean, I'm jist newly up here.'

'We'll hiv tae see whit we can dae aboot that then, eh?'

Before I could reply he said, staring at two young females pushing their way up to the bar, 'Wull ye look at them – they're smashers. Dae ye no' think so? I fancy the wan in the green jumper. The ither's no' bad either.'

'I suppose so,' I said. He pushed back his chair and informed me that he was going to the bar for another pint, adding, 'Amongst ither things.'

'Get me wan while ye're at it,' I called.

'Sure,' he said, moving away with a rapt look.

I didn't mind being left alone. I was tired and didn't want the bother of chatting up birds, since I can only do that after I've had around five whiskies. I suspect I lack finesse even then, but at that stage I don't care.

A man sat down beside me and asked if the seat was taken. I shook my head. I didn't expect Jimmy back for a while. He set his pint tumbler on the table. It was almost empty. 'I'm glad to sit,' he said. 'I hate standing at bars.'

I replied, 'I know whit ye mean. I canny be bothered gaun up there for anither pint either.'

He looked at my tumbler, also almost empty. 'Don't worry,' he said, and called on a guy collecting the glasses. 'Get this lad a pint of beer, Alec, and one for myself at the same time.'

'Right, sir,' said Alec.

'I didny know ye could get served at the tables,' I said.

'You can't really,' said the guy, tilting the chair as he leaned back. He added with a superior smile, 'Only those and such as those can.'

I was prepared to sneer at his upper-class style, the handlebar moustache matching the colour of the grey locks combed fashionably onto the well-cut collar of his well-cut suit, but he looked so much at ease and friendly with it that I could only say, 'Thanks. I'll get the next round.'

'Don't bother, young man. I won't be stopping long.'

I grimaced. 'I know. This place is a dive.'

He raised his eyebrows and said, wagging his finger at me, 'But it's not really. I like this place. They serve a good pint.'

For some peculiar reason I was reminded of the guy with the moustache in the ancient poster who states that your country needs you. When the beer arrived he watched me closely as I took the first swallow. To please him I smacked my lips, wiped the froth from them, and told him it was a good pint.

'You're right, young man,' he said, as if I had passed a test.

'Do me a favour,' I said, retaining an amicable expression, 'Don't call me "young man". Where I come from it disny go doon well.'

'And where is that?'

'The west coast.'

'Ah, the west coast. A fascinating area with its rivers, lochs and mountains, and the people so friendly. I'm surprised you left it.'

'It's no' sae fascinatin' where ye're on the dole.'

'Ah, the dole.' He tapped his teeth and sighed. 'A dreadful situation.'

'At least I've a job here,' I said. 'So I'll be OK.'

'I would guess,' he said, searching me with his eyes, 'that you are an outdoor worker.'

I showed him the palms of my hands still calloused from my last period of work. 'That widny be hard tae guess. I'm a brickie.'

'And I'm a travelling salesman,' he said.

'That's a helluva thing tae be,' I said, feeling cheated that he had turned out to be a mere traveller. 'Thank Christ I'm a brickie.'

He finished his beer and said, 'You're right, young man. Travelling is a dreadful occupation. I'm thinking of giving it up.'

He brought out a card from his pocket and handed it to me saying, 'If you feel lonely or simply in the need of a chat with someone, such as myself, in a quiet pub, call in at this place after eight o'clock. My name is Colin Craig.'

With that he was gone. The card read: THE OPEN DOOR, 2 LANTERN LANE. OWNER MICHAEL MCLERIE, LICENSED TO SELL BEER AND SPIRITS.

Jimmy returned carrying two pints of beer. 'Who wis that?' he asked.

'Naebody in particular. Ye took yer time.'

He smirked and drew two curves in the air with his hands. 'You should have seen these birds.'

I stared ahead bleakly as we sipped our drinks. Jimmy was casting anxious glances towards the bar. I sensed I was spoiling his evening, but I had no inclination to chat up birds, particularly on the strength of three beers.

'I'm gaun away soon,' I said. 'It's been a tirin' day. If ye're wantin' tae get back tae the bar, don't let me haud ye.'

'Are ye sure? I could get ye fixed up easy wi' a bird.'

'Maybe anither time.'

'Aye, maybe,' he said, giving me a doubtful glance.

CHAPTER 2

The building site was muddy and damp on the feet, particularly if your boots let in.

'Ye'll need wellies,' said Jimmy as I stood poised, searching for a dry patch to leap upon.

'I've nane.'

'See the ganger, then.'

He squelched off in his sturdy boots.

'Wellies!' said the ganger when I approached him about this.

'I wis telt ye supplied them.'

'It depends on how long ye've been on the job. We don't

haun' them oot straight away.' He looked in the direction of my feet concealed by mud. 'Ye'd think ye've never worked on a site afore. Ye should ken whit gear ye need when ye start.'

'It wis hard frost when I left hame,' I explained. 'I didny think I'd need them.'

He stroked his moustache. His eyes brooded upon me as he said, 'Ye'll jist hiv tae buy a new pair, then.'

'I canny afford tae buy nothin' until I get ma wages.'

'That's typical!' he said. 'You folk come up here expectin' everythin' laid on. It's nae good enough.'

'I didny expect a' this abuse because I asked for a pair o' wellies.'

We faced each other. My eyes became strained with giving him the fixed stare.

He said, looking away, 'If ye don't like it ye know whit ye can dae.'

I replied, 'Only when it suits me.'

My feet embedded in the mud were freezing. I believe I would have walked off there and then if I could have easily extracted them. I can usually tell on my first day if I'm going to stick the site. Already the odds were stacked against this one.

'Is that so?' he said, his eyes bulging. 'If it suits me ye can collect yer books.'

'Hiv ye no' heard o' the Employment Protection Act?'

His eyes lost their bulge. He said with a trace of humour, 'Dae ye no' ken there's nae protection onywhere nooadays,' and walked away.

Jimmy left the cement mixer to ask what had happened.

'He said there's nae wellies.'

'Ask him next week. He's always moody wi' new starts.'

'I might no' be here next week.'

'Hing oan.'

A few minutes later Jimmy returned with a pair of wellingtons. 'They wir lyin' in the hut,' he said. 'They're no' new but they're better than nothin'.'

I began to lay the brick, slowly at first. The clay was rough on my fingers. My shoulders ached from lack of practice. Gradually I became more adept and was working at a fair speed when one of the labourers stopped to watch.

'Hopin' to make a big bonus,' he said.

My concentration faltered. I turned to him saying, 'Maybe.'

'Ye michny be popular wi' the rest o' the squad.'

'Bugger the rest o' the squad.' I turned my back and spread the mortar. I wished he would vanish, but he remained, gawping.

'Wan o' the new starts?' he asked.

I laid down my trowel and wiped my hands on a piece of rag. 'Seems an unpopular thing tae be.'

I faced him to see he was a wee thin man, neither young nor old nor disagreeable looking. He wore a loose jumper over a pair of baggy flannels.

'Och naw, laddie,' he replied. 'It's normal tae be a new start but don't tire yersel' oot straight away. It's a long day, ye ken.'

'Ye widny have a fag tae spare?' I asked.

'I'll gie ye a roll-up. I've nae use for these ither cork-tipped things.'

He brought a tobacco tin from his pocket and rolled me a smoke. As we puffed we studied a bit of wall I had built. 'Ye're daein' fine,' he said.

The day wore on and I felt a great need to eat the rolls and cheese Danny had wrapped up for me in a newspaper.

'Whit's the time?' I asked an apprentice working further along the wall.

He didn't hear me. I thought maybe he was deaf. Apprentices often are. I moved nearer to him and repeated the question.

'How should I ken?' he said.

I noticed his top layer of bricks was uneven. 'That's aboot as straight as the Rocky Mountains,' I pointed out.

'Mind yer ain business.'

'It is ma business. I don't want the bloody wa' hauled doon because you canny build straight.'

He turned to say something unpleasant no doubt and bumped against the structure. The bricks scattered. I pulled him clear and slid on the mud. A brick struck me on the temple.

'Are ye a' right?' he said, wide-eyed as he bent over me.

'Jist gie us a haun' up.'

My head throbbed and felt sticky when I touched it. Two workers arrived on the scene and escorted me to the hut, with the apprentice close at my heels still saying, 'Are ye a' right?'

Inside the hut I was told to sit down and have a fag. A mug of tea was shoved into my hand. The place filled up with workers, most of them stationed beside the electric kettle. The ganger entered and looked round the hut. 'Whit's a' this?'

'The apprentice built his bricks slack and they fell doon.'

'The new fella copped wan on the heid.'

The apprentice was shoved in front of the ganger, his face extremely pale. 'I didny mean it,' he said.

'Don't worry aboot it, I'm a' right,' I told him.

The ganger roared at him, 'Get oot ma sicht!' and the apprentice slunk out the door.

'Where's the first aid kit?' asked the ganger.

'I didny know there wis a first aid kit,' said someone.

'There wis wan here a month ago, and if it's no found somebody's gettin' hauled ower the coals.'

I thought their search would be useless. I've never seen a first aid kit in any site, unless you counted a bottle of aspirins left by a labourer I once knew who used to swallow them along with Barr's Iron Brew as a substitute for booze. A tin of plaster was found under a bench. With a serious expression the ganger applied it to my cut and wiped it with a rag. When he stood back to survey his handiwork another cup of tea was placed in my hand. 'For shock,' said the donor. The ganger turned to stare at the group of men standing close to the electric kettle, drinking tea.

'Ya bloody skivers,' he roared. 'Ye're fifteen minutes aff the tea break. Are yez on strike or somethin'?'

The wee guy with the baggy flannels stepped forward and said, 'Here, take this tea, Geordie, and gie us a' a break.'

The ganger said nothing; his moustache twitched. Slowly he sipped from the mug of tea, as if he was judging a rare wine. We all watched him open-mouthed. Then he said, 'Ye've put too much bloody sugar in it.'

Everyone relaxed and took down their pieces from the shelf. Jimmy rushed in breathless as we sat chewing away. 'Whit's happened?' he asked.

'Nothin' much.'

He stared at my sticking plaster. 'I heard ye were hurt bad. I've phoned for an ambulance.'

'An ambulance!' spluttered the ganger.

'The apprentice telt me he wis hurt bad,' Jimmy was saying, when someone shouted in the hut door that there was an ambulance coming up the track.

'Run oot quick and tell him it wis a hoax,' said the ganger. 'Afore ye know it we'll be havin' the polis in. We don't need that, dae we?' he added, addressing me.

'Naw,' I said, doubtfully. 'It's no' as if I'm supposed tae make a claim, is it?'

'There wid be nae point in daein' that.'

He then informed me that he would try and get me a new pair of wellingtons for Friday, which was the earliest he could manage, since he had to order them. I said that was fair enough.

'Dae you know,' said Jimmy to the lodgers when we were back at the digs waiting for our dinner to be served, 'the apprentice would hae been a goner if it wisny for the lad here. Saved his life he did, and nearly copped it himsel'.'

I shook my head to dispute this statement, automatically touching the sticking plaster on my temple.

'Nae wonder ye look pale,' said Dad. 'Are ye feelin' a' right?'

'I'm fine.'

Actually I felt squeamish and unable to face any food.

'Mind and gie this guy a double helpin',' said Jimmy to Danny when he was hurling the trolley over. 'He needs it efter riskin' his life.'

'Is that so,' snapped Danny, slinging over my plate. 'Well I risk ma life every day staunin' ower bilin' pots and pans and naebody cares.'

I took one look at my helping of boiled cod and potatoes and headed for the bathroom.

'Ye're no' sleepin', are ye?' Jimmy's voice broke into a dream I was having where I floated above rooftops like a barrage balloon ready to burst.

'Whit time is it?' I asked, sitting up, dazed.

'Time ye were oot enjoyin' yersel'.'

'I don't feel sae good.'

He pulled at my wrist. 'Get up quick. I can hear Danny comin' up the stairs. Ye're no' supposed tae be in bed wi' yer boots on.'

By the time Danny walked into the room I was on my feet, stretching and yawning.

He said to Jimmy, 'Ye've nae right bein' in here. It's nae your room.'

'Whit's the big deal aboot that?' I asked.

'The big deal is that we don't want lodgers traipsin' aboot places they've nae right tae be in. It's the rules, ye ken?'

'I didny know aboot that rule,' I said to Jimmy. 'Did you?'

'Fine he knows,' said Danny. His gaze fell on the bed. 'Will ye look at that black mark –' he began, but we were out of the room and running down the stairs two at a time.

The streets were empty and warm for a change. We strolled along with hands in pockets, passing some pubs on the way. I had no cash so I had to keep passing them. Jimmy was strangely silent. At last I asked, 'Where are we gaun?'

'D'ye fancy meetin' a lassie?'

'It depends,' I said, after thinking about it.

Well, I've got a date wi' wan o' the lassies in the pub yon night. She said she'd bring her pal along for you; a nice quiet lassie, seeminly, real class.'

'Ye mean the ither wan that wis in the pub?'

Naw. This wan doesny like pubs, frae whit I hear.'

I explained that I preferred to get my own dates, plus the fact that I was gasping for a pint.

'But they're waitin' for us. I hope ye're no' gaun tae back oot.' As I started to lag he added, 'There they are staunin' by the picture hoose. Look, they're wavin' to us.'

He crossed the road. Reluctantly I followed. Only one of them had waved. The other was intently scanning the photographs of the film stars inside the glass frames on the wall. He introduced me to the one who had waved. She was a dumpy blonde with a pug nose named Jean. She giggled when I shook her hand. 'That's Nancy,' she said, pointing to her friend who looked round from the photographs and gave me a cool nod. I put my hand in my pocket, deciding that there was no future for me with this skinny dame, even if she was passable looking in a snooty way.

'Right then,' said Jimmy, assuming a grin as we stood around staring at each other awkwardly. 'Noo that we're acquainted where dae ye think we should go?'

When no one answered he said, 'Whit aboot the pictures?'

'We've seen them,' said Jean.

'So have I,' I said, and caught the eye of the tall dame called Nancy. She gave me an uncertain smile which I was obliged to return.

'We might as well take a dauner through the park,' said Jimmy with a defiant look all round.

'Might as well,' said Jean. She grabbed his arm and they walked away so quick they almost ran.

'Dae ye fancy a stroll?' I asked Nancy.

'I suppose so,' she said.

When we entered the park Jimmy and Jean had disappeared. I felt uncomfortable and noticed I was walking too fast. This dame could barely keep pace with me. I ventured to say, as I slowed down a bit, that it was a fine night.

'Yes,' she said.

To fill in the silence I began to whistle on one low note as dreary as the morse code. When I stopped I heard her sigh. I wondered if I should feign a sudden attack of migraine as an excuse for a quick departure. It would appear feeble, though, if not insulting. It might be better if I ran over the hill flapping my arms like a rooster about to take off. Then she would think I was a genuine nutcase and be glad of her narrow escape.

'You remind me of a boyfriend I once had,' she said, breaking through all this conjecture. 'He was a Canadian and always whistling, imitating birds. He said it reminded him of the backwoods of Canada.'

'I've never been tae Canada, let alane the backwoods.'

'It was nothing to do with Canada really,' she said. 'It was the whistling.'

I didn't know how to answer this. I could only say vaguely, 'Maybe you still miss him?'

'Why do you say that?'

'I don't know why. Maybe I look like him. How should I know?'

I was becoming annoyed with the subject and felt like telling her this when she said, 'Actually you're much better looking than him.'

Being heartened by this comment I asked her if she would like to take my arm, which she did; and we walked over the hill, still not saying much but feeling a lot happier. At least, I was, and I think she was. As we travelled I was pressed with an urge to kiss her; but how could I? I hardly knew her and couldn't think of any way to accomplish this intimacy. She suddenly stopped walking when we were near a tree.

'It's a fly,' she said. 'It's in my eye.' Right enough the place was thick with midgies.

‘Let me see,’ I said. She gave me her handkerchief, which was lucky for me since I never carry one or even possess one. With a bit of manoeuvering I managed to ease the mangled insect out, wiping the water from her eye in a most natural fashion, which made it easy for me to kiss her without any awkwardness.

‘Yer hair smells like fresh cut grass,’ I said afterwards, burying my face in her curls and blessing the midgie that gave its life in such a good cause.

‘It’s only Sunsoft shampoo,’ she said.

‘It’s the nicest shampoo I’ve ever smelled. I could inhale it a’ night. It’s as good as chloroform.’

‘Don’t be stupid,’ she said, pushing me away. ‘You hardly know me.’

‘Whit’s that got tae dae wi it? I feel as if I’ve met ye somewhere afore in a different time.’

‘I don’t believe in reincarnation,’ she said, laughing.

I tried to kiss her again but she backed off and said that she preferred to walk. I didn’t mind this because she still held on to me. For the sake of a subject I mentioned the Canadian guy, which was a mistake. She said that he was none of my business, then withdrew her arm.

‘I’m sorry,’ I said, stopping to light up a fag, ‘but ye shouldny have spoke aboot him in the first place.’

She walked quickly on ahead. I became angry. I shouted, ‘Seems tae me ye’re still keen on him if ye’re takin’ it that bad.’

She flounced back and slapped my face. Her action was so unwarranted it made me laugh. ‘Ye must be some kind o’ screwball,’ I said. She would have lashed out again if I hadn’t caught her wrist. She struggled feebly when I told her that I might as well kiss her again whether she liked it or not, since she was going to be angry whatever I did or said.

‘That’s not true,’ she declared, and let me kiss her without making any move to get out of it.

‘Are you satisfied now?’ She was smiling. I thought she had a very nice face, thin, with a turned-up nose and green eyes that sometimes looked yellow, depending on the light.

'No' really,' I said.

We carried on kissing and cuddling for a while. I would have liked to do more than that, but didn't want to risk angering her. I decided she wasn't really a screwball, but I sensed that she was unpredictable to say the least.

I told her a bit about myself, explaining why I'd left my home town to come here for work. She raised her eyebrows and said that it was a shame I had found this so difficult. For her part she'd never had any bother finding work. She had worked in the same office as a typist since leaving school.

'Dependin' on who they are,' I said, trying to keep my voice free of irony, 'some folk have no problem.'

'But I know it can be difficult nowadays,' she assured me.

The subject trailed off and I thought it just as well not to pursue it. By this time I liked her so much I wouldn't have cared if she was a top class model. Then she said, 'It's getting dark. The park gate will be closing soon.' So we hurried back and the gate was still open.

'I'll have to go anyway,' she said.

I didn't want to argue with her, but I asked if she would meet me tomorrow night outside the park gate.

'I don't know,' she said. 'Why not make it Saturday?'

'Let's make it the morra night.' I thought that by Saturday I could have faded from her memory.

She hesitated, then said, 'All right, tomorrow night.'

Before I could say any more she was running towards the bus stop across the street from the park, and had caught the bus as it was drawing away. With her free hand she waved back to me.

CHAPTER 3

'Whit's happened tae Dad?' I asked. We were all sitting at the kitchen table. The space which he usually occupied had been empty for a few days.

'Dad comes and goes like the weather,' said the guy beside me. 'Ye never ken whit thon wan's up tae.'

Henry Bell, a big slow-speaking chap who was a street sweeper, said, 'I'm sure I saw him on a park bench lyin' under a bundle o' newspapers.'

'Is he a tramp then?'

Jimmy laughed, 'Aye, wan that can eat wance a week at the Station Hotel.'

'Whit does he dae for a livin'?'

'Onythin' and everythin'.'

Another guy said, 'I think he's a salesman. Mind that time he wis sellin' encyclopedias.'

'Ye mean he took the deposits,' said Jimmy. 'Naebody ever got wan.'

I asked, 'Did ye gie him a deposit?'

'Naw, but I've known them that has and are still waitin' for the encyclopedia.'

'Wance he wis takin' photies,' said Henry Bell. 'I gave him a deposit for wan he took o' me.'

'Did ye get the photie?'

'No' yet,' said Henry wistfully.

Someone else said, 'He's got nae sense o' heilan' pride.'

'Is that some kind o' breid,' said Henry Bell, grinning like mad. We all looked away from him.

Later, when I was studying my face in the bathroom mirror in an anxious way, someone kicked the door and shouted, 'Wull ye be long?' I ignored the thumps for a while. It's normal for guys to pound at the bathroom door and use any pretext to get you out.

Finally I unlocked it to face Jimmy, who said, 'Jean wis on the phone to say that Nancy canny make it. It seems she's got a cauld, but she'll see ye on Saturday, if she's better.'

'I couldny care less,' I said. 'She wisny ma type.'

'How are ye lookin' sae angry then?' said Jimmy, following me into my bedroom.

'I'm no' the least bit angry. By the way,' I added, 'ye're no' supposed tae be in this room. Ye know the rules.'

'Don't take it oot on me,' said Jimmy, 'jist because a bird gave ye a dizzy.'

He was leaving so I said, 'OK. I'll no' take it oot on you if ye lend me a fiver. That'll be twelve I owe ye, and I'll buy ye a drink intae the bargain.'

We walked through a dingy back street to what Jimmy described as a joint where I was bound to meet a bird to my taste. I did not fancy this idea. Inadvertantly I put my hand in my pocket and brought out the card given to me by the toff with the handlebar moustache. I showed it to Jimmy and said on the spur of the moment, 'I've jist remembered I wis to meet a guy at this place in connection wi' a business deal. Dae ye want tae come?'

'Whit kind o' business deal?'

'I'll let ye know when I get there,' I said, hurrying on while Jimmy studied the card. Now that I had some money I wasn't caring whether he came or not, but I was determined I wasn't going to be palmed off with another bird.

He ran after me saying, 'I think I've been there wance. It's a wee auld fashioned dive wi' nae lounge and nae juke box.'

'As far as I'm concerned that'll make a chinge.'

'I don't really fancy it,' said Jimmy but he kept pace with me all the same.

We travelled over cobbled pavements which scuffed the tips of our footwear. It didn't bother me since my boots were well scuffed already but Jimmy said, 'This is murder,' examining his black casuals. It was a long street of archaic three-storey tenements. Women hung over their window sills, surveying the packs of kids and dogs belting up and down the pavements. One black hound leapt on Jimmy, slavering with friendship. He aimed it a kick, a mile wide fortunately.

'Leave that dug alane,' a woman shouted from her window, 'ya cruel midden! Then to the dog, 'Come awa' up here, Sheba.'

With a glance of regret at Jimmy it bounded up a close, followed by three canine admirers.

'We shouldny have came here,' said Jimmy. 'This place is a cowp.'

'I never forced ye tae come,' I said. 'Anyway, it's your toon, no' mine.'

We arrived at an area of wasteground, deserted apart from a cat sniffing into a pile of rusty cans. Ahead were the crumbling remains of a tenement.

'How much further?' I asked.

'See yon wee buildin' alang at the end?' said Jimmy, pointing.

'At whit end?'

'At the end o' this buildin'. It's a wee place a' by itsel'.'

'Oh aye,' I said, unable to see anything. However, we came to a wee hovel of a place with a sign above the entrance which read The Open Door.

'It is a right pit, innit?' I said.

'I warned ye,' said Jimmy.

Inside the place looked no better. It was distempered in a shade of brown like the colour of dried blood. A naked bulb hung from a low ceiling. Some drab male figures were pressed against the counter and the barman on the other side surveyed us suspiciously from deep-set eyes.

Jimmy whispered, 'Whit did I tell ye?'

'It's got atmosphere,' I said, and ordered some beer and whisky from the barman in a loud and cheerful voice to convey that I found nothing amiss with either him or the pub. If the guy called Colin Craig had found it quiet and friendly, who was I to doubt it?

'Is yer name McLerie?' I asked the barman, and to prove I had a sound reason to drink within these walls I added, after showing him the card, 'I'm only enquiring since a guy called Colin Craig gave me this and telt me to look him up in here. Dae ye know who I mean?'

He shook his head and returned the card. 'I've never heard o' him,' he said, and didn't mention whether he was the owner or not. He flashed me a warning look and disappeared through an opening behind the bar.

'Definitely friendly,' said Jimmy.

'So, he's never heard o' him. Whit does that prove?' I said, and began to study the four bottles of Red Hackle whisky on the shelf above the bar. I asked a guy standing on my other side if it was the only brand they sold.

'Who dae ye mean by they?'

'The owner for example. Is he no' the guy that's servin'

called McLerie?'

'I never kent that wis his name.'

He stared at me owlishly through his specs, looking like the school dunce with his cloth cap resting on his ears. He explained that he hadn't a clue about anything that had happened recently, such as the names of new pub managers, because he had been in bed all winter with the gastric flu. I looked beyond him to the guy at his back, also wearing a cloth cap, though the fit was better.

'Dae ye know a guy called Colin Craig who drinks in here? Tall guy wi' a moustache and speaks posh,' I asked him, mainly to impress Jimmy who was sipping his beer with a martyred expression.

The second guy with a cap thought this over and asked if this Colin Craig wore a kilt.

'I don't know. He hudny one on when I saw him.'

The guy next to me said, 'It's big Eck who wears a kilt. Have nothin' tae dae wi' that yin for he's a violent man. Kicked a hen tae death while he wis waitin' for a bus.'

I was going to ask if the hen had been waiting for a bus as well, but the other guy interrupted to say he had heard big Eck had killed his own dog for watching him eat his dinner.

'I doubt it's the same guy,' I said, and informed Jimmy from the side of my mouth that we were in the presence of loonies. Immediately he stated loudly that we shouldn't have come here anyway, especially as there was no juke box.

'Never mind the juke box,' I said. 'If ye don't like it ye know whit ye can dae.'

Sullenly he threw a fiver on the counter to pay for the next round. The guy standing next to me informed me in a sincere manner he was sorry that he could not place this man called Craig, then stared hard at the fiver. I told Jimmy, again from the side of my mouth, to buy the loonies a drink. It was as well to have friends in the place. He complied with an even more sullen expression. After that I stood, leaning with one elbow on the bar, watching the barman pass up and down with his face as austere as a grand master of the

Orange Lodge being introduced to the local priest.

Then Jimmy nudged me. 'Will ye look at that!'

I turned to see a man standing further along the counter. I thought at first he was wearing a mask, the pink and white plastic type used by guisers at Halloween, but on closer inspection I saw he was a burnt-out case, maybe caused by the war or a car crash. His face was definitely a re-modelled job.

'That's a bloody shame,' said Jimmy. 'Dae ye think we should get him a drink?'

'The guy'll be used tae his condition. Ye don't want tae embarrass him.'

'How should that embarrass him? The wans beside ye wereny embarrassed.'

'Don't talk sae loud,' I whispered and gave the cloth-capped ones a nod and a smile to which they responded by a lift of their tumblers. In order to change the subject I said to them, 'It's no' a bad pint in here.'

'Oh, indeed, aye,' said the guy next to me, smacking his lips. He enquired if I was from these 'pairts'. I explained that I was from the west coast, naming the county. He informed me that he had a sister living in the same county by the name of Mary McPherson. He wondered if I knew her.

'I don't think so . . .' I began to say, when Jimmy thrust his face between us and stated, 'I know the McPhersons well. I went tae school wi' them. Whit did ye say her first name wis?'

The guy recoiled and mumbled, 'McPherson is her married name.'

'So, maybe I went tae school wi' her man. Whit's his name?'

I gave Jimmy a dig in the ribs and told him to forget it. I explained to the other two guys who were looking confused, 'The fact is, we're in here waitin' on this Craig guy. We know naebody at a' except for him, and ma mate here doesny even know him.'

'And I don't particularly want tae,' said Jimmy.

It was at this stage I put my hand in my pocket and

brought out some loose change. 'I'm skint,' I declared.

'And I've only enough left for fags,' said Jimmy.

The man beside me in the cloth cap said, 'I wid buy yous a pint, but I'm a bit short too.'

'Especially wi' him bein' on the sick,' said his pal. He added, 'But I'm sure McLerie would gie you a pint on the slate.'

'I thought ye didny know the barman's name?'

'I knew his name. It wis ma freen' here that didny.'

McLerie, who must have been within earshot of all this, came over and said to the guy beside me, 'Did I here you asking for tick?'

'Not at all,' said the guy, pointing towards me, 'it's him that's wantin' it.'

McLerie studied me from his suspicious deep-set eyes, then surprisingly asked me what I wanted.

'Two pints and two haufs o' whisky,' I said quickly. 'I'll pay ye first thing Friday when I get ma wages.'

'I'm sure you will,' he said, with a touch of sarcasm, but he poured out the drink hurriedly as if he had a lot on his mind, then vanished into the back premises. Jimmy and I wasted no time in emptying our glasses. We left the pub without any kind of farewell to the cloth-capped guys. They had lost interest after we had been served, as though they had done their duty.

I said to Jimmy when we were outside, 'A' the same it wis queer, him lettin' us drink on the slate. He didny look friendly and he didny even know us.'

'I think he wis jist wantin' rid o' us,' said Jimmy.

'I think you're right,' I said. 'And ye know whit – I think he wis wantin' rid o' us before Craig came in.'

'Could be,' said Jimmy. 'Maybe he thought we were plain-clothes detectives tailin' the guy.'

We both laughed at this idea. Jimmy stepped on to the wasteground which was now covered two inches thick with mist, explaining that he was going to have a slash. I was about to do likewise when someone tapped me on the shoulder. I turned to face the burnt-out case. His face shone waxen in the moonlight.

'Jesus Christ,' I said, reeling back with fright. 'Whit the hell dae ye want?'

'I wis gaun tae ask,' he said in a quavery voice, 'if I could walk alang wi' ye a bit. It's a quiet road and I get nervous by masel'.'

'Nae problem,' said Jimmy. 'We'll see ye're a' right.'

The burnt-out guy then placed himself between us holding on to each of our arms for support.

'Is yer eyesight bad as well?' I asked.

'It's no' that bad, but ma feet are.' He continued plaintively, 'I hope I'm no' ony bother.'

We both assured him that he wasn't any bother, but I wasn't happy with the situation. He seemed to be leaning all his weight against me, and was heavier than if he had been drunk and incapable. I tripped over his feet. 'Help ma God,' he shouted, hopping on one foot with great agility. 'That wis bloody sore.'

'Sorry,' I said. 'I'm no' used tae walkin' sae slow.'

Jimmy addressed me. 'You should watch whit ye're daein'.' Then he broke off to exclaim, 'Christ almighty!' which wasn't surprising. The burnt-out guy appeared to be peeling the skin from his face.

'Ye mad bastard,' I shouted. 'Whit's the game?'

I calmed down when I looked into the mild grinning face of Dad, dangling a rubber mask.

'Ye very near gied me a heart attack,' said Jimmy. 'Ye were worse lookin' than the phantom o' the opera. Whit's the big idea?'

'It's like this,' said Dad, after giving one or two quiet chuckles. 'I'm testin' masks for a theatrical company. I thought I would try this one oot in the pub to see if it looked real. I think it worked well enough.'

We assured him that it had worked very well. Then I asked him if he had left his digs.

'No' exactly. I owe three weeks' money, but I'm no'

botherin' aboot it meanwhile.'

He broke off to say that he heard we were skint and if we wouldn't be offended he was prepared to give us a fiver. 'Ye can consider it a wee loan,' he said.

Jimmy said he would sure appreciate it. I asked him how he knew we were skint. Did McLerie tell him?

'As a matter o' fact he did,' said Dad, handing me a fiver. 'We sometime get on the talk now and then.'

'At that rate,' I said, surprised that McLerie talked to anyone, 'maybe you'll know a guy called Colin Craig?' and I gave him a description.

After a pause Dad said, 'I believe I have seen such a person, though I never knew his name.' He went on, 'Wis it somethin' urgent ye wanted him for?'

'How should it be urgent?' I asked. I had the feeling Dad knew Craig a lot better than he made out, but I wasn't concerned. The important thing was that we had enough for another couple of drinks.

'No reason at all,' said Dad. 'Except that I wis gaun back tae McLerie's later since I can get a doss on the floor for nothin'. If I had seen the guy ye were referrin' tae I could have passed on a message.'

'There's nae message,' I said, as we waved him goodbye.

After Dad had vanished into the dark I said, 'That's the queerest thing I've ever come across.'

'Whit's that?' asked Jimmy.

'A guy testin' masks for a theatrical company. Who'd be sae daft as tae dae that?'

'I know whit ye mean, but Dad's no' sae daft, though he's got a' these queer occupations. I widny be surprised if he's workin' for the polis and the mask is tae disguise himsel' in places where he's known.'

'At that rate I'll be giving him a wide berth,' I said.

'On the ither haund,' said Jimmy, 'maybe no'. Maybe he's just eccentric.'

'Aye, maybe.' I thought that Dad was one very devious guy, but I was pleased with his fiver.'

CHAPTER 4

Somewhere in the city we heard an explosion which shook the top layer of our bricks. We wiped the sweat from our brows and stepped back to survey the wall. It was hot and for once there was no wind to cool us.

'Whit the hell wis that?' I asked.

'Maybe a gas pipe burst.'

'Sounds like dynamite.'

'Maybe war wis declared and we never heard.'

'Or some o' them political bampots. It's no' the first time they've planted a bomb.'

We all lit up a fag. Benny, the wee thin guy with the baggy

flannels, said, 'It wis in the paper a couple o' weeks back that fuse wire wis found in a plastic bag near an oil tank.'

'Imagine blawin' up an oil tank,' said the apprentice.

Benny said, 'Personally speakin', I think somebody wis jist stealin' fuse wire and drapped it.'

'There's terrorists everywhere nooadays,' said Jimmy. 'It's the new craze.'

'Plantin' bombs is no' new,' said Benny. 'Look at Guy Fawkes.'

'He wis whit ye call an anarchist,' said the apprentice.

We all stared at him deliberately wide-eyed. He added sheepishly, 'So I heard.'

'I bet you don't know whit an anarchist is,' said Jimmy.

'Is it no' somebody that's against the government?' asked the apprentice.

'At that rate we're a' anarchists.' said I.

'Look oot,' said Jimmy. 'Here comes Hitler.'

The ganger, who was actually called Butler, came up to us and said, 'Is there somethin' wrang wi' yous lot? Ye're staunin' aboot as useless as a crowd o' female geriatrics at a beauty competition.'

Jimmy explained, 'We're jist seein' that the wa's steady efter that explosion.'

'Whit explosion?'

'Did ye no' hear a big bang as loud as when the landmine drapped on Fermer Watson's field during the war?' said Benny.

'Naw, I didny,' said the ganger. 'I don't even mind o' Fermer Watson, never mind a landmine.' He ran his hand over the wall and stated, 'These bricks are gey slack.'

'We're tryin' to tell ye, there wis an explosion. That's how they're slack.'

'And I'm tryin' tae tell ye,' said the ganger, 'that if this job is no' up tae scratch you'll a' be aff this site quicker than craws aff a dyke durin' target practice.'

Benny hitched up his trousers aggressively and stepped in front of the ganger. 'Dae ye no' think ye're gaun ower the score talkin' like that. There's nothin' wrang wi' the wa'. Maybe ye want rid o' us so as ye can get in yer masonic pals.'

'So that's whit it's aboot,' said Jimmy ominously.

In a grim manner we all moved one step nearer the ganger, including the apprentice. The ganger, give him his due, did not budge an inch, apart from the bulge of his chest and eyes.

'Ya ignorant shits,' he said. 'It's nothin' tae dae wi' the masonic or ony ither faction. It's tae dae, first of a', wi' the new architect, who's been complainin' aboot everythin' tae the new manager, who's got his orders frae the authorities to cut back everywhere so they can save money for the big shots at the tap o' the tree, who appear to feel a draught blawin' through their wine cellars these days. That's whit it's aboot.'

There was silence for a moment. Then I said with a nervous laugh, 'I thought this wis a boom toon.'

'Maybe that wis the boom ye heard then,' said the ganger. He added, addressing me personally, 'And anither thing, yer protection act ye mentioned is no' worth a damn noo. They've made anither act which states that the buildin' trade is tae be streamlined; in other words haufed in two doon the middle. Nane o' us is protected, includin' masel'.'

With those mighty words he ambled off like an elephant heading for its last resting place. Jimmy said, after a gloomy pause, 'I'm gled o' that.'

'Gled o' whit?'

'Gled that he'll cop it alang wi' us when the time comes.'

'I wouldny bank on it,' I said.

'He's only a worker like oorsels,' said Benny.

'Anither thing,' said the apprentice. 'They canny sack me because I'm supposed tae serve ma time nae matter whit happens.'

Jimmy gripped the apprentice by the neck of his tee-shirt. 'Jist you shut yer face and gie us wan o' yer reefers. I've seen you smokin' the hash through a hole in the bog door. We a' know ye're a junky.'

The apprentice wriggled free. 'It's nothin' tae whit I've seen you daein' through the bog door!'

He backed away while we all grabbed Jimmy to keep him off the apprentice.

'Tell us, son,' we asked, 'whit does he dae in the bog?'

'Nothin',' he shouted, and ran towards the site hut.

'Goes tae the bog and does nothin',' I said, amazed.

'Maybe it's constipation,' said Benny.

Jimmy said, after we released him, 'That apprentice is wan o' the cheekiest swines I've met.'

Later that afternoon the ganger handed out the pay packets.

'I suppose you'll a' be gettin' fu' tae the gills,' he said. We all nodded except the apprentice.

'Whit aboot yersel'?' I asked him pleasantly.

'I gied it up years ago. It's a mug's game.'

Benny said, 'Man canny live by breid alane. Ye need tae blot oot yer worries at least wance a week.'

'It's still a mug's game.'

I tore up my pay packet, counted the notes, stuffed them into my hip pocket and tossed the empty packet away.

'Pick that up,' said the ganger.

'Whit for. It's empty.'

He shook his head. 'Have they nae idea how to act where you come frae? Tossing litter doon like that.'

I turned my head away to hide the disdain in my eyes. The ganger tapped my arm and said, 'Try and screw the heid at the weekend, particularly wi' the booze.'

'It's nane o' your business whit I dae at the weekend.'

'Maybe so, but keep in mind that ony guy who's no' in sharp on a Monday is paid aff. Too bad if it's no' due tae a hangover for it's taken for granted that's the reason.'

By the time I got back to the digs after having a few pints with Jimmy and paying him the money I owed, as well as paying the landlord his dues, I felt tired and unwanted. Everyone was going out, except me.

After the meal of fish and chips – something of a treat to give Danny his due – I retired to the lounge and fell asleep in front of the television. When I woke up the room was empty. I stared at the television for some time, trying to work up enough energy to stand up, but I must have fallen asleep again. The next apparent thing was the sound of Danny switching off the set.

'Nae point in wastin' electricity,' he said.

'Whit time is it?'

'Time ye were in yer bed by the look o' ye.'

He was almost right. The clock on the mantelpiece said eleven. The lodgers should be staggering in any minute, with a carry-out I hoped. Then I remembered that the rules of the house cancelled this out. The night was truly dead. Perhaps it was just as well because Jimmy tip-toed into my bedroom later to inform me, with fumes of beer blowing over my face, that Nancy had told Jean to tell Jimmy that she would meet me at the park gate on Saturday.

'This is really a nice place, don't you think?' said Nancy, as we sat in The Cosy Nook licensed restaurant. 'It's so clean you could eat off the floor.'

I handed her back the menu card informing her that I wasn't hungry. After a week of Danny's stodgy dinners my stomach felt it was due a rest.

'I'll jist have a drink,' I said.

'But it looks funny if you don't order a meal,' said Nancy.

'I'll have some scrambled egg then.'

'It's not on the menu.'

I beckoned the waitress and asked if I could have a drink to be going on with since I couldn't make up my mind about the food.

'Have you any scrambled egg?' asked Nancy.

'We haven't,' said the waitress.

'So, I'll jist have a drink in the meantime,' I said again, and ordered a double whisky.

'Bring me a martini,' said Nancy.

When the waitress was gone I said, 'I thought you were havin' somethin' tae eat.'

'I'm not eating alone. It looks funny.'

I studied her across the table. Her hair was arranged to look like feathers and her lips shone like pink icing. I thought she looked great, even though her face was screwed up. When I complimented her on the spotted green blouse she wore, she said, 'It's an old one,' and shifted her gaze along the room to another young couple who sat clutching long amber glasses. They seemed depressed, perhaps on account of the Val Doonican record playing in the background. When the whisky arrived I swallowed half of the glass straight away, partly because I had waited a long time for it, partly to offset the weight settling on my brain. Nancy asked, after she had taken a sip of her martini, if I usually drank so fast.

'Aye,' I said, and tossed back the other half.

The waitress returned and asked if we'd made up our minds about what to order.

'The fact is,' said Nancy, 'my fiancé is on a diet and can only eat scrambled egg, so there's no point –'

'That's right,' I broke in. 'I'm under doctor's orders.'

'Don't worry about it,' said the waitress. 'But if you come in on a Wednesday we'll have scrambled eggs then.'

'Since we can't order food we might as well leave,' said Nancy, closing the menu card with a sigh.

'Do you know,' I said when we were outside, 'I hate scrambled egg.'

Nancy began to giggle. 'How you managed to say you were under the doctor's orders I'll never know.'

She continued to act in a light-hearted way and I ceased to be depressed.

'Have you always worked on a building site?' Nancy asked.

We were walking through the park. If we had been sharing a wee bottle of booze the situation would have been perfect. I knew that was out of the question, but I was happy enough.

'If ye mean since I left school, aye.'

'Is it hard work?'

'Hard and mucky.'

'Why don't you do something else then?'

'I don't want tae. Anyway, I'm lucky tae have a job.'

'I suppose so.' She added, 'I've never been out with anyone who worked on a building site.'

'How does it feel?'

She gave me a diffident smile. 'Uncomfortable sometimes.'

I was cast down again. It occurred to me she found me uncouth, which I knew I was. I began to brood on the Canadian, who had likely been a very suave guy.

'What's wrong?' she asked, after we had walked a good while and I had remained deliberately silent.

'If ye find me so uncomfortable why are ye here?'

'You take everything very seriously.'

'Not always. In that restaurant you were the serious one because I didny want tae eat.'

'I see,' she said quietly. 'You're now going to pick on trivialities. You shouldn't have had that double whisky.'

'You think I'm drunk because I had a double whisky?'

'I don't think you are drunk, but a double whisky can influence your judgement.'

'You don't say?' I said sarcastically.

At that point we came to a halt, not far from the tree where we had kissed before.

'If you're going to be like this I might as well go back home,' she said.

'You might as well since I make you feel uncomfortable.'

'I really detest you,' she said. Her face was red and angry. When she drew back with her fists clenched I grabbed them and said, 'Let's chuck it. Ye know I'm crazy aboot ye.'

She struggled for a bit, then finally calmed down. I pulled her under a tree and we kissed long and satisfactorily. We were very compatible when kissing.

Afterwards she said she thought she had a temperature

and I asked her if that explained her bad moods. 'You are the most inconsistent dame I've ever known,' I told her.

'I bet you haven't known many.'

'That's true.'

'I'm not surprised,' she said, 'you've no manners.'

I wasn't bothered when she said this. I had no wish to be like the Canadian, who likely had plenty of manners.

'That wasn't the problem,' I said. 'My mother wanted me tae be a priest, but I couldny gie up the booze.'

'Liar,' she said. 'You're not even a Catholic.'

I tickled her under the arms. She laughed as if she was enjoying it. We were acting like kids, but I think we were never so happy as at that moment. Then she told me a bit about herself. For instance, how her parents were from her point of view old-fashioned – particularly her mother, who worried about appearances, and what the neighbours said, and keeping up with the Joneses. 'You know what I mean,' she finished.

'I know whit ye mean,' I said, thinking about my mother, who mainly worried about paying the rent and buying the grub, apart from worrying about me, which she said she did all the time. I spoiled everything by changing the subject and asking Nancy if she loved me better than the Canadian.

'It's none of your business,' she said, drawing back and assuming the untouchable look. I lit up a fag to conceal my chagrin. Then she said that she was cold and wanted to get home because she didn't feel well. We walked back through the park in silence. When we reached the gate where she caught the bus I asked her if she would see me the next afternoon at the same place. She sighed and said all right in a sullen manner. She allowed me to kiss her, but her lips were cold.

CHAPTER 5

On Sunday afternoon I sat on a bench inside the park watching young lassies dance in a circle as they sang, 'Here we go like birds in the wilderness, birds in the wilderness, birds in the wilderness. Here we go like birds in the wilderness on a wet and windy morning.'

I was reminded of my first day at school when I had stood snivelling with humiliation in a similar circle. It was queer how the song had cropped up again after all these years, like a bad omen. I moved on, but not too far, so that I could keep my eye on the park gate for Nancy. A crowd had gathered in the valley below, some standing and some sitting, in front of a big wagon altered to make a stage, on which three guys wearing check shirts were strumming guitars in an experimental fashion. It was a busy scene and one I hadn't bargained on. A guy approached me holding a collection box. I shoved in some change and asked what it was all about.

'It's aboot peace,' he said.

'Peace?'

'Aye, the peace festival.'

I moved on down the hill and sat on the grass at a spot where I could be seen from the path above if Nancy showed up. I was beginning to have my doubts. She was fifteen minutes late judging by the town hall clock which struck every quarter of an hour. When another fifteen minutes had passed and the guitarists were playing in earnest, I gave up hope and lay back with my arms under my head wondering if the pubs were open on a Sunday afternoon, yet not really caring too much.

A voice from behind shouted in a gravelly tone, 'Hiv ye a match on ye?'

I looked round to see three mature guys sprawled on the grass, obviously sozzled. A fourth lay on his back snoring. The question was repeated by a man with a threatening look on his face, which could have been merely a slackening of the facial muscles caused by too much booze. I flung over my box and he asked if I wanted a 'swally' of the South African wine bottle he held up before me.

'We're a' freens here,' another one assured me, wiping the sweat from his brow. They must have been roasting in their dark greasy suits.

'I might as well,' I said.

I swallowed as much as I could before the bottle was taken from me, then I pointed to the snoring man. 'He could get sunstroke.'

'No' him', said the guy who had asked for the matches. 'He's immune frae a' the elements on account o' his brain cells bein' deid.' He attempted to light his shag roll-up which was bent in two different angles.

'Have a fag,' I said, and handed round my packet, hoping for another swig at the bottle when everyone had had their turn.

'Big crowd here the day,' I said conversationally. 'I'm telt it's a peace festival.'

'Peace!' said another guy. 'That's a bloody good yin.'

He winked at no one in particular and took a long pull at the bottle. He might have finished it if the man on the grass hadn't sat up and grabbed it off him.

'Ya bastards,' he said, 'there's hardly ony left.' Then he looked at me and asked, 'Who the fuck are you?'

I thought he was a man who looked better asleep. Awake he appeared mean-faced and cross-eyed. At first I wasn't sure if he was talking to me or the guy beside me. However, the guy beside me answered. 'He came ower and sat beside us, Wullie, and put the bottle tae his mooth afore we could dae a thing aboot it. That's how there's hardly ony left.'

'Is that so,' said Willie. He transferred the bottle to his right hand and held it by the neck in the manner of a weapon.

'Don't worry, I'll get anither one right away,' I said, rising to my feet. He advised me to hurry up and bring some shag while I was at it.

'Sure, Wullie.'

'Make it two bottles,' said the guy with my matches safely in his pocket.

'Sure, I'll make it three.'

With that and a careless wave of the hand I was off down the hill. The beer tent loomed up before me, which was handy. I was in the mood for a pint.

Inside two customers stood drinking beer at a table laden with heavy tumblers. One of them said, 'Help yersel' tae the beer. The guy in charge is away for a piss. I'm takin' in the money.'

The other one said in a clipped accent, 'Possibly he drank too much of his own beer,' and wiped his handlebar moustache lightly with the back of his hand. This guy was

Colin Craig, the toff whom I had met in the pub; the man I had pretended to be looking for in The Open Door. Now I really was glad to see him. He looked friendly and I was lonely.

'How's it gaun?' I asked.

'Remarkably well,' he said. 'And you?'

'Smashin'.'

His companion, who had a face as sharp as a blade, informed me that he'd hardly sold anything from his stall so far and that it was a particularly mean crowd out there who would sooner put ten pence in a collection box than buy one of his lovely Honolulu tee-shirts. He went on, giving me a sharp look to match his face, 'Ye widny like wan? I've got a great selection, only three quid each.'

'No thanks,' I said.

'Or some jewellery for the wife or the girlfriend bein' selt for next tae nothin'.'

I lifted a pint tumbler of beer and looked at the thin-faced guy blankly when he held his hand out for the money. Craig shoved his hand down, saying sternly, 'This lad is a friend of mine who has come all the way from the west coast to find work.'

'Is that near the Gallowgate?' said the other one with a sniff.

'Only as the crow flies,' I said.

We all laughed and moved outside, carrying our tumblers. 'I thought you had to collect the beer money,' I said to the sharp-faced guy.

'I've got ma ain business tae attend tae,' he said, and pushed off through the crowd, who were swaying to the rhythm of the guitarists. At that moment I pined for Nancy.

'By the way,' I said to Craig, 'McLerie telt me that he'd never heard o' ye. I visited The Open Door, at your suggestion if ye mind, but ye never showed up.'

'Please accept my apologies. I usually round off my evenings in that pub but there's the odd time I don't. As for McLerie, I can't account for his attitude. He's a strange fellow, and very secretive. He may have thought your interest in me was suspicious. I'll have a word with him on this score.'

'Anither funny thing,' I said, 'is that Dad, wan o' the lodgers where I stay, knows ye as well. I met him in The Open Door.' Inconsequentially I added, 'Wearin' a false face, tae.'

'Of course, Dad!' said Craig after wrinkling his forehead for a second. 'A wonderful character. Yes, I know him very well.'

'Seems a strange coincidence,' I said, thinking for the first time how strange it really was.

'Not at all,' he said reprovingly. 'There is no such thing as a strange coincidence. There is only such a thing as a coincidence, but if it bothers you –' He broke off and shrugged, as if to imply he was prepared to end our association if I felt bad about it.

'It doesny bother me,' I said. 'I've made a few pals since I met ye last. McLerie and Dad's nothin' tae me and coincidences don't bother me either.'

Craig raised his eyebrows and said, pointing his head in the direction of the guitarists beating it out loud on the stage, 'Wonderful music,' but twisting his mouth as if he meant the opposite. I nodded and told him curtly I was away to look for my bird since she was the reason for me being here in the first place. I placed my empty tumbler on top of a post and left him, to make my way through the folk standing thick and stubborn like cattle. I collided with a guy coming in the opposite direction. He reeled back and fell into a wee space between the bodies. I helped him up before he was trampled into the ground.

'Ye'll no' get through there,' he said, 'it's the lottery wheel.'

I turned back and found Craig standing on the same spot. The last note of the guitarists' number was vibrating on the air.

'Did you not find your bird?' he asked cautiously.

'I couldny get through the crowd. I wis too late onyway.'

A voice spoke through the microphone, loud but indistinct. 'I'm not in the mood for this,' said Craig. 'Let's go somewhere.'

'The beer tent?' I suggested.

He shook his head and stared about restlessly. I asked him if he was looking for somebody.

He shrugged. 'Not exactly. Like yourself, I'm too late.'

'I'll tell ye whit,' I said, concluding that this man was as lonely as myself, 'how aboot gettin' somethin' tae eat?'

Craig took out his wallet as we waited beside the snack van. I told him that I would pay but he was already handing the money over to the guy serving the hamburger rolls. I noticed the initials on the wallet were A.R.B. It occurred to me he was a pickpocket, but it scarcely interested me. I decided I would ask him about it later, if it began to bother me.

'Let's eat at the top of the hill where it's quiet,' he said.

I agreed to this readily because there was the faintest of possibilities that Nancy would be waiting, desperately scanning the crowd for me, but of course when we got there she wasn't.

'It's a pity,' said Craig as we wiped the grease from our fingers, 'that your friend didn't arrive. I could tell you were upset about it.'

'I'm no' botherin',' I said, adding ruefully, 'It's only one o' these things that can alter yer life, I suppose.'

After a pause he said that my life was more likely to alter if I did something about it rather than wait passively for things to happen.

'How d'ye mean?' I asked.

He looked me straight in the eye and said, 'I can't make any promises or even say very much at present, but I have been making some plans to start my own business, and I will need to hire some good men.'

'If you're offerin' me work,' I said, 'I'm obliged tae tell ye that I only like bein' a brickie.'

'That's all right, young man,' he said, patting me on the shoulder. 'You are as well to do what you are happiest doing. Money isn't everything.'

'What kind o' work were you referrin' to?' I asked. 'I can always change my mind for a higher price, dependin' on whit it is.'

He laughed. 'Already I have said too much. In a few weeks time I can be more explicit.'

'I canny be bothered wi' vague promises,' I said. 'I widny like tae think that ye're havin' me on.'

'Then don't think it, young man,' he stated, and said no more about it.

From the same bench I'd sat on when I'd arrived in the park, we looked down on the scene below. The crowd had thinned. Kids and dogs ran about unchecked. Folk were drinking openly from beer cans. Some were drunk and staggering. There was no sign of the sozzled guys I had spoken to, except for the empty wine bottle lying a few yards away. The same guy was speaking through the microphone.

I said, 'You'd wonder how anyone bothers tae speak through a microphone – it's obvious naebody's listenin'.'

'There's always someone who is.'

'But ye know the words aff by heart. No more war, love thy neighbour and ban the bomb. Naebody seems tae care.'

'Except the man on the speaker.'

'That's right,' I said. 'Except the man on the speaker.'

A wind sprang up and blew empty crisp bags and paper cups over the grass. Folks stood shivering, shouting on their kids and dogs, then cramming things into plastic bags. The guitarists were back on the stage belting it out with gusto, but the day was finished; the mood was gone. A church clock struck five.

Craig said, 'The hotels should be open soon.'

I fixed my thoughts on the promise of booze, though I couldn't help mentioning to Craig as we left the park that my bird's hair smelled of fresh cut grass. I asked him if he thought this was an unusual perfume. He said that it was one of his favourites.

CHAPTER 6

'That wis some carry oan, last night,' said Jimmy.

We were eating our breakfast and I was pushing aside a plate of porridge.

'Whit's wrang wi' it?' Danny asked, pointing to my plate.

'Nothin', but it brings me oot in heat spots.'

'I'll take it,' said one of the lodgers. He worked in a sawmill and had two fingers missing from his left hand. They called him 'the gannet' or sometimes 'the hoover'.

'I hardly got a wink o' sleep,' said Jimmy.

'That wis terrible,' I said, shoving my plate towards the sawmill worker.

'So ye' mind o' kickin' open ma door and punchin' the wa', then sittin' on the edge o' ma bed for ages?'

'I don't mind anythin'.'

'Ye were in a bad state. I'm sure Nancy couldny have been pleased.'

'Do me a favour,' I said. 'Don't mention her name to me and if ye ever see her tell her to keep oot ma road.'

Unintentionally I had raised my voice and everyone was looking over at me. Danny shouted from the kitchen sink, 'Did ye get a dizzy, then?'

'You jist mind yer ain business and get a move on wi' the tea,' I shouted back.

'Did she no' show up?'

'That's of no consequence beside the sore head I've got at this moment,' I said coldly.

'I wonder why she never showed up,' said Jimmy, regarding me thoughtfully. I shut my eyes.

After drinking my tea and nibbling apathetically on a bit of toast, I told Jimmy to explain to the ganger that I had contracted a severe bout of diarrhoea and wouldn't be able to start work until dinner time. Then I went upstairs to my room, lay down on the bed, and immediately fell asleep.

I was awakened by Danny's aggrieved voice calling in my ear, 'Ye've nae right tae be in bed at this time in the morning.'

I sat up slowly and regarded him with loathing. 'At whit time can ye be in bed if ye're no' feelin' well?'

'It's nothin' tae dae wi' me if ye're no' well. It's ma job tae see everybody's oot the rooms afore I clean them.'

'How can ye no' dae the room later? I might feel better then.' Stupidly I threw back the cover to expose my boots to his shocked countenance.

'That's the maist disgustin' sicht I've seen. Ye'd better get oot this room afore I tell ma Da.'

'Wait a minute,' I said as he headed for the door. 'If ye let me lie for another hour I'll gie ye a pound and I'll take ma boots aff as well.'

He paused and turned. 'I canny,' he said. 'If they find oot they'll ask questions.'

'Who'll ask questions?'

'The polis.'

'The polis? You must be jokin'.'

'I've got ma orders tae report onythin' unusual that happens wi' the lodgers tae the polis. Lyin' in bed wi' yer boots on when ye should be at work is definitely unusual.'

'Ye're a crazy bastard,' I said. He stood studying me like a gigantic mole, with his eyes beady and his long nose twitching. I became angry and leapt out of bed, I stood close to his gangling body and said, 'Why should the polis be watchin' me?'

'Nae reason,' he said, backing away. 'I wis jist sayin' that to get ye up. There's nae need to go aff yer heid.'

'If I think onyone's spyin' on me,' I said. 'I'll render them incapable wi' ma haunds roon' their throat.'

Danny gulped and said, 'I'll tell ye whit, make it two pounds and ye can stay in bed for an hour if ye take yer boots aff.'

'Ye're no' sae crazy,' I said. 'Take this pound and beat it before I really lose ma temper.'

After he left I didn't take my boots off, or shut my eyes, or even yawn. I was so wide awake it was painful. I felt uneasy, guilty and ashamed for no good reason – a familiar state after I've drunk to excess, particularly if it is accompanied by loss of memory, and even more particularly when I've been dumped by a bird I am crazy about. I grabbed my jacket, walked out of the room, down the stairs and into the kitchen, where Danny was emptying rubbish into a bin.

'Fetch ma pieces,' I said as he regarded me open-mouthed. 'I'm gaun tae work.'

When I was collecting my tools out of the site hut, the ganger entered. I explained while he lit his pipe that I felt a lot better than I had done earlier, so I had decided to show my face. He continued to puff with his eyes on the floor as though his thoughts were far away. When I headed outwards he said, 'Haud on.'

I turned to him with raised eyebrows and he added, 'Ye canny start at ony time ye happen tae fancy, ye ken.'

I said in a reasonable manner, 'But there wis nae way I could have came earlier considerin' I had a dose of the skitters in the first place and you are aware of whit the toilet facilities are like here in the second place.'

'So it wis the booze?' he said.

'It definitely wisny the booze for I hardly touched it a' weekend.'

'That's no' whit I heard.'

We stared hard at each other for a minute, then I said less reasonably, 'I don't care whit ye heard.'

'Is that so,' he said, pointing the stem of his pipe towards me. 'Well, ye were telt that onyone no' in sharp on a Monday gets paid aff.'

'For Christ sake. I wisny well. Deduct the lost time aff ma wages if it'll make ye feel better.'

He didn't answer so I thought I'd change the subject. 'Did ye get me a new pair o' wellies?'

He shook his head. I became angry and told him I was going to report him to the foreman on a matter of victimisation, but he remained unperturbed, puffing and blowing his pungent smoke in my face. I walked out and banged the door hard enough to loosen its hinges. When I joined the rest of the squad I was deliberately silent.

'Whit's wrang wi' you?' the apprentice asked. 'Did somebody pinch yer lollipop?'

Jimmy said to the apprentice, 'Ye'd better no' talk tae him. He had a dizzy at the weekend and hell hath no fury like a man wi' a dizzy.'

At that moment I made up my mind I was going to pack in the job on Friday and return home. The folk up here were all hustlers. The place wasn't fit for a dog.

'Hey,' said the apprentice, 'don't lay these bricks sae fast. It's no' as if I canny keep up wi' ye, but I don't particularly feel like it.'

'Fuck the lot o' ye,' I replied in an explosive manner, startling the apprentice who dropped the bricks from his hod, which gave Jimmy the excuse to curse him strongly. He hadn't forgiven him for the hole in the bog door incident.

'Leave him alane,' I said. 'It wis ma fault.'

We all picked up the bricks and Benny asked me if I felt better now. I wasn't sure if he was referring to the state of my bowels or my bad mood, but I nodded anyway. Jimmy offered me a fag. I took it and said, 'You want to keep yer big mouth shut.'

'How's that?'

'Ye telt the ganger I wis on the bevvy last night.'

'Whit makes ye think that?'

'How else wid he know?'

'It stauns tae reason he wid say that if ye were in late. If yer leg wis hingin' aff he wid say it wis because o' the booze.'

I had to admit to the truth of this and pointed out to Jimmy that I wouldn't have been on the booze if Nancy had shown up.

He shrugged, 'So these things happen. It's no' the end o' the world. You'll likely see her afore the week's up.'

'No' me,' I said firmly.

When I returned to the digs, Danny handed me a white envelope. Inside was a typed message which read, 'I WILL SEE YOU OUTSIDE THE CINEMA AT SEVEN O'CLOCK AND WILL WAIT THERE FOR TEN MINUTES ONLY. YOURS SINCERELY, NANCY.'

I was overjoyed by this brief communication.

'Is yer nose botherin' ye?' I asked Danny, who was trying to read the words upside down, but there was no malice in my voice. I felt sorry for the lonely bastard. He hadn't even got a bird, never mind a bird like Nancy. When he was slinging the plates round the table I told him that his cheese pie looked great.

'Makes a chinge frae yer usual opinions,' he said stiffly.

Afterwards I studied my reflection in the bathroom mirror and thought that if I didn't purchase some new gear soon my clothes would fall apart. I could follow Jimmy's advice and put down a deposit with a city tailor for an outfit and if I left the area I needn't bother about the rest of the payments. According to him guys were always doing this. In the meantime I had only enough money for fags. It appeared I had blown most of it on Sunday's escapade. I didn't even remember having a good time and I suspected I hadn't. It was just as well Nancy wasn't a bird with expensive tastes. I was grateful to her on that score alone. I unfolded her crumpled message, which struck me now as being a bit too brief. She could at least have apologised for not keeping the date, or even explained why she hadn't. On reading between the lines of the neat typing I detected some indifference. Perhaps I shouldn't go. If I had any pride I wouldn't. On the other hand, when I thought it over, I knew there was no way I wouldn't go.

'Ye're a sicht for sore eyes,' said Jimmy when I bumped into him coming up the stairs.

'Whit dae ye mean?' I asked, aware of my threadbare condition.

'Am I supposed tae mean somethin'?' he said, wide-eyed and debonair in a bright yellow pullover.

'I don't like yer tone o' voice. It's insinuatin'.'

'Insinuatin'?' he repeated angrily. 'The trouble wi' you is ye've got wan big chip on yer shoulder. Ye want tae knock it off or ye'll have nae freens left.'

As I slowly descended the stairs I thought perhaps he was right, but I wasn't caring about friends just then. I only cared about Nancy, and felt dismally aware of how little I had to offer her.

'Have you been waiting long?' said Nancy. She had arrived breathless outside the cinema, as if she had been running, which I considered a good sign.

'Naw,' I said. Actually I'd been waiting for fifteen minutes.

'I bumped into someone I knew,' she said. 'I couldn't get away.'

'I see,' I said, feeling dampened. Curtly I asked what had happened to her on Sunday.

'Oh that,' she said. 'I had one of these terrible headaches when all you want to do is lie in a darkened room.'

'And did you?'

She drew me one of her looks. 'Of course. What do you think?'

I decided to pay her back. 'I wis late yesterday. I met a guy on the road tae the park and we had a couple o' jugs. I wisny sure whether you'd been and gone.'

'I'm glad your day wasn't wasted,' she said quietly.

I studied her from the side of my eye. She looked as sensational as a model from a clothing catalogue. She wore an olive green dress that touched her slim figure in all the right places. Her arms and legs were bare and brown.

'You'll catch cold,' I said as an excuse to stroke her arm.

She laughed, 'Then you'll have to lend me your jacket.'

Apart from a few can rings and paper cups on the grass, the park was cleared of Sunday's litter. A faint imprint of tyres marked the place where the wagon turned into a stage had stood.

'That's where I was wishing you were here,' I said, pointing to the imprint.

'Probably drinking,' she said.

'Whit else could I dae?'

She became serious. 'I wish you didn't drink so much.'

'I wish I didny need tae.'

I confessed as I took her hand that I hadn't been late at all. In fact I had been too early and had waited for a long time for her before I had taken a drink and when I had it was only beer. I told her also that if I thought she felt as much for me as I did for her I wouldn't need to touch another drop of liquor again.

'How much do you feel?' she asked, smiling.

'Let's go somewhere quiet and I'll show ye.'

We lay on the grass in the shelter of some bushes. Her head rested on my shoulder. Slowly and imperceptibly we moved our positions until she lay under me. I asked her if I was too heavy. She said that I wasn't. Later I asked if I was hurting her and she shook her head. At least I thought she shook her head. By this time I was in such a state of exaltation that I was incapable of being sure of anything.

Afterwards I said I was sorry. I hadn't meant to hurt her or do anything like this. I had only intended to do some heavy kissing.

'You didn't hurt me,' she said, then sat up and began to comb her hair. It was incredible how composed she was, as if nothing had happened.

'Ye know I'm crazy aboot ye,' I said.

'Crazy?' she said, with a rueful smile.

'I love you then, if that's any better.'

'Just as well,' she said. 'I don't do this sort of thing with anyone.'

It was on the tip of my tongue to ask her if she had done it with the Canadian, but I only just refrained.

She began to shiver. 'I'm cold,' she said. 'Let's walk.'

'Can I get a smoke first?' I asked. 'It's a well-known fact ye always have a smoke afterwards.'

'But I don't smoke,' she said.

'Ye'll have to learn, because we might do it again.'

I was only joking, but her face became set. 'You can stop and have a smoke if you want, but I'm walking on.'

'What's wrong?' I asked, when I caught up with her after I had lit up. When she didn't answer I asked, 'Wis it yer first time?'

'No,' she said, looking at me, her eyes disturbed. 'Maybe that's the trouble.'

I didn't want to aggravate her with questions. I said, 'If it's any consolation it's no' ma first time either.' This was a lie.

CHAPTER 7

The sun shone over the building site, drying the mud on our boots and forcing us to throw off our shirts as we wiped the sweat from our brows.

'They say it is to be like this a' weekend,' said the apprentice.

I nodded at him amiably and accepted one of the reefers which he now displayed openly. He confided that he was going to be the owner of a second-hand motor bike.

'I hope ye can drive it?'

'I'll be OK. I've had plenty shots o' ma cousin's.'

Benny said, 'And I hope ye're no' gaun tae become one o' them Hell's Angels.'

'I'll never be good enough for that,' said the apprentice.

'Ye don't have to be a' that good on a bike,' said Benny. 'So long as ye know the Hitler tunes, and better still if ye join the National Front.'

'I think I'll join them then,' said the apprentice.

Jimmy said, 'I've a nephew who ca's hissel' a Hell's Angel and he's a quiet fella.'

'So he will be,' said Benny, 'until he gets on his bike and aff wi' his pals tae beat up the Jews.'

'As far as I ken he only goes roon' the ring-road and there's nae Jews there.'

'That's only as far as you ken. It doesny have to be Jews. It can be Italians, Pakkies, or the tinkers; in fact, ony bugger that walks across their path.'

'How the tinkers?' asked the apprentice.

'If ye wereny sae ignorant you'd ken that in Europe they're called Gypsies and Hitler got rid o' them alang wi' the Jews.'

'I hope,' said Jimmy, addressing Benny, 'ye're no' suggestin' that ma nephew's a Nazi.'

'There's nae difference between them and the National Front.'

'I wish tae Christ I hudny mentioned aboot the motor bike,' said the apprentice.

I said to Jimmy, 'I widny be surprised if Dad is one.'

'A Hell's Angel?'

'Naw, somethin' mair in the line o' a National Front member. Look how he walks oot the ludgings withoot sayin' a word to anybody, then shows up a few days later as if he'd never been away.'

'Whit does that prove?' said Jimmy. 'He's always been like that.'

'And that false face business. That wis weird if ye ask me.'

Benny said, 'I dinny ken the guy yous are talkin' aboot, but here's somebody comin' who's definitely weird.'

It was the ganger delivering the wages. We turned to our bricks while he pondered long upon us. After a time Benny looked round and said as if surprised, 'Why, it's yersel', Geordie, wi' the pay pokes, and a welcome sicht ye are.'

The wages were handed round in grim silence, which was normal for the ganger, so it came as a shock when he handed me mine and said, 'Ye're on a week's notice.'

I shoved the envelope in my pocket and turned back to the bricks, uncertain if it was his idea of a joke, though he wasn't in the habit of joking. He said, dispelling my uncertainty, 'They're cuttin' back the men. I warned ye a while back.'

'So ye did,' said Benny, 'but there's plenty work. We're a' needed, even the apprentice.'

'I've got ma orders.'

'Are ye sure ye've got yer orders?' I asked. 'Or wis it jist yersel' that wanted rid o' me.'

'If ye don't believe me, see the foreman.'

'When dae we ever see a foreman?'

By now he was heading back to the hut with his usual elephantine gait.

'That's rotten,' said the apprentice, breaking the two minutes silence after he had gone.

'I'm helluva sorry,' said Benny.

'It's pure shit,' said Jimmy. 'I'll have tae dae the work o' two brickies.'

I handed him the brick I had lifted. 'Ye can start wi' that one then.'

'I heard the firm's changin' haunds. We'll a' likely go eventually,' said Benny.

'They'll no' get rid o' me, surely,' said the apprentice, after taking a deep draw of his reefer.

Benny said, 'Listen, son, they can dae whit they bloody well like.'

'It seems to me,' Jimmy said to Benny with a red angry face, 'that you ken a lot mair than I dae, and it seems to me as well that you and the ganger are gey pally at times. I wouldny be surprised if ye're baith tryin' to get rid o' me.'

'Aye, and me tae,' said the apprentice.

Benny shook his head. 'I wis never pally wi' Geordie in a'

the twenty years I've kent him, and he kens that if you don't.'

I interrupted. 'Ye'd think it was yous that were gaun instead o' me.'

'I ken, son,' said Benny apologetically. 'This is whit happens when there's a pay-aff. It causes a bad atmosphere wi' the ones that are left. Maybe you're the lucky one, bein' well oot o' it.'

'Sure,' I laughed. 'I'm the lucky one.'

'I'll tell yous something,' said the apprentice, startling us all by the extra loud way he spoke. 'I've been thinkin' how I've never had a kind word aff ony o' yous since the day I started. Wait and see, I'll be the next to go.' He then blew smoke in our faces.

Jimmy said, 'Ye want tae chuck that stuff. It makes ye imagine things.'

I asked the apprentice for a last draw of his reefer. He calmed down and handed it over, telling me to keep it if I wanted.

'We'll a' have a wee puff,' I said, and passed it round.

Benny coughed after he took his draw and said, 'Man, that stuff fair chokes yer lungs. I dinny ken how ye can smoke it.'

'There's a knack tae it,' said the apprentice mournfully.

We continued to take draws until the reefer was finished. Benny said that the hash made him tired. I said that I felt no different.

'That's because you don't inhale it deep enough,' said the apprentice.

He was probably right because the pupils of his eyes were like pinpoints, and he looked stupefied.

'Ye'd better pick up yer trowel afore ye drap aff tae sleep,' said Jimmy to the apprentice. 'Yer eyes are as squint as ma first piss.'

When they all lifted their trowels I told them I might as well get going since I was paid off anyway.

'But we'll see ye next week,' said the apprentice.

'That's right,' I said, but I knew I wouldn't. No one ever

works a week's notice in the building trade.

Back at the lodgings I informed everyone in a loud and cheerful voice that I had been paid off and so I would be going back home. I smiled to convey how pleased I was by this turn of events.

'Whit dae ye want tae go hame for?' asked Henry Bell. 'I could get ye a start at sweepin' the roads.'

'When?'

'Efter the fair holidays.'

'I canny wait that long. I feel hamesick.'

'Don't forget to pay yer dig money,' said Danny, who had been listening to all this with his arms folded.

'I'm no' gaun away right this minute,' I said. I surveyed my plate of stovies. 'A' the same, it's an ill wind that blaws nae good.'

Dad, who had only recently returned to his place at the table, said, 'Maybe I could get ye a start wi' Sanderson's Soft Shoe Polish. They'll soon be needin' folk tae pass roon' the leaflets.'

'I'll think aboot it,' I said, with a sidelong glance at his mild, friendly face.

After swallowing some forkfuls of the stovies I passed my plate over to the sawmill worker, who accepted it with a grateful nod and said that he would be sorry to see me leave.

I asked Jimmy, 'How's aboot comin' alang tae the pub for a quick one? I'm chokin' for a drink.'

'I'm meetin' Jean in a wee while.'

'It's only for a quick one,' I said. 'Somethin' tae stiffen ma nerve when I tell Nancy that I'm fired.'

'I thought ye wereny botherin'.'

'Nancy will be botherin'. Ye know whit dames are like.'

'I'm sorry,' said Jimmy. 'I widny trust masel' to get one drink. I'd end up gettin' bevvied.'

'Never mind,' I said, and headed quickly for the outside door. I caught up with Dad, who had left the lodgings some minutes before me in his usual unobtrusive manner. 'Fancy a drink?' I asked.

'Actually I've an appointment tae keep.'

'No' at The Open Door, surely,' I said, adding with a sarcastic titter, 'wi yer false face on.'

He smiled politely, 'No' this time.'

'Anyway, I'll get ye alang the road a bit,' I said.

'If ye like.'

I sensed by the way his lips were clamped together he was dying to get rid of me. I felt angry at his sudden change of attitude, so for spite I mentioned that I'd heard someone say he was a member of the National Front. His only reaction was to raise his eyebrows and state mildly that folk were capable of saying anything at all to break the monotony. Then without warning he crossed the road and skuttled round the side of a building like a beetle heading for its den. I carried on, passing some pubs but reluctant to enter them in case their clients were partisan to certain causes I had no notion of. I thought it best to head for The Open Door. I had retained a good impression of the place. McLerie was a kindly man when he gave strangers credit. If I ran there and back I would be in time to meet Nancy at the park gate. There were minor considerations like not having washed or shaved and reeking of beer, but surely she would understand that a couple of drinks is the first thing a man needs when he's paid off.

There was a moment as I stood outside the pub, breathless, when I considered turning on my heels. Perhaps it was a premonition of something unpleasant in store for me, but that is not unusual and seldom deters me. Perhaps it was simply that I knew there was no time for drinking and I was blowing my chances with Nancy if I did, and me crazy about her too. Despite it all I walked straight in and ordered a double whisky and a pint. McLerie served me with a face of stone, so I said to him quickly, 'I believe I owe ye some money?'

His nod was barely discernible. After I paid him and he looked no happier, I asked if he thought Colin Craig would show up this time, adding with an edge to my voice, unless he still hadn't heard of him. He ignored this statement and informed me in a pointed way that he was closing early because he was auditing. My head spun with this information, plus the double whisky I had swallowed in one gulp.

'Ye're auditin'?' I repeated with disbelief.

'That's right. We're auditin'.' His sunken eyes bore into mine.

I became angry and called to a customer further along the counter, 'Did ye know that this pub is closin' early because they're auditin'.'

The guy shuffled his feet and told me it was all one to him as he was going shortly, and to prove it he threw back his beer and left. I could still catch Nancy yet, I thought, as I banged my glass on the counter to convey I wanted to be served. McLerie shot up from behind the counter like a jack-in-the-box.

'Anither whisky,' I said, 'and I'll be leavin' ye tae yer auditin'.'

'There's nae immediate hurry.'

Now he sounded more irritated than anything else. This encouraged me to order another whisky, and then another one, and another one. After that I became stoned. I stood with one foot on the brass rail running round the bottom of the counter, staring in stupefaction at the customers surrounding me, who appeared to have emerged from the walls. I think I was happy at that stage. McLerie approached me and accused me of being drunk.

'I'm no' surprised,' I said, laughing at the idea of being drunk and the sight of McLerie's angry face.

I don't remember much of what happened after that until the moment I awoke lying on the floor of the back room in the pub. The place was scarcely big enough to swing a cat. Most of the space was occupied by a wooden table, around which sat McLerie, Dad and Colin Craig. They were staring at an open ledger, and paid me no attention when I struggled up from the floor to sit on a chair beside them, feeling sober but ill and thinking if I could get just one short alcoholic drink I would feel better. Craig was running his finger down a page in the ledger.

'It's not bad, what we've got here, and in fact it should be enough for the first payment,' he said.

'So long as it looks good on paper,' said McLerie.

'Let's hope there's nae hitches wi' this Lifeline deal,' said Dad.

I sat as still as I could in order not to disturb them. They were an ill-assorted trio: Craig the toff, McLerie the sinister pub owner, and Dad the shabby lodger. I judged them to be villains of some kind, perhaps about to bump me off for intruding. I was wondering whether I should make a run for the door when Craig turned towards me and asked civilly if I felt any better. Immediately I apologised for any bother I might have caused and explained that usually I didn't pass out so easily.

'It was probably one of Michael's Mickey Finns,' said Craig with a mocking look in the direction of McLerie, who continued to look stern. I don't think the man was able to smile.

'Ye widny have a drink tae spare?' I asked. 'I'm parched.'

Dad pointed to an old jaw-box sink displaying one tap covered in verdigris. 'Help yersel'.'

'It's no' that kind o' parchedness.'

'Fetch a bottle of rum,' said Craig, giving me a wink, which reassured me further.

'I don't know why I should,' said McLerie, 'and I'm damned if I know how he's here listenin' tae everythin'.'

'Because I said so,' stated Craig and banged the ledger shut.

'There's nae harm in the lad,' said Dad. 'He's up here on his ain and he's lost his job.'

I decided that if they were villains, at least they were friendly ones, and being friendly is what counts.

'You've lost your job already?' Craig asked.

'When it comes tae a pay-aff the foreigner's always the

first tae go,' I pointed out.

'That's true,' said Craig. 'Don't worry. I'll get you fixed up somewhere.'

His words, said so casually, gave me a great feeling of warmth and security, which wasn't diminished when McLerie said, as he placed four glasses and a bottle of rum on the table. 'Next thing ye'll be cuttin' him in.'

'Don't forget we can always do with a strong fellow,' said Craig.

'Can ye drive?' Dad asked me.

'Aye,' I said happily, wondering if they were smash and grab jewel thieves and I was to drive a getaway car.

'Whit dae we need a driver for?' asked McLerie.

'I dinny ken,' said Dad, 'but it's always handy tae know.'

'Well,' said Craig, holding up his glass, 'here's to a prosperous future.'

'You bet,' I said.

In no time at all, and without any revelations being made as to the manner in which I was to be fixed up, the bottle was finished and we were out on the pavement while McLerie was locking the door.

'Ye're no' a' gaun away,' I said with dismay.

'We've got an early start if some folk haveny,' said McLerie in his usual surly fashion. Drink had made no difference to his mood.

'True,' said Craig. 'I'm afraid we'll have to be on our way.'

'But whit aboot me?' I said, panicking. 'I thought ye were fixin' me up.'

'Don't worry,' said Craig, looking over his shoulder as he walked away, his face a blur in the twilight. 'I'll be in touch with you through Dad.'

They were all walking away and my legs were buckling under me. The fresh air on top of all that I had drunk was like a shot of chloroform.

'Aren't you coming?' Craig called.

'Walk on,' I groaned. 'I feel sick. I'll catch up wi' ye.'

I leaned against the pub door for support, automatically searching in my hip pocket for my wage packet, which is a reflex action on my part no matter how drunk I am. My last conscious thought, before I slid down on to the step, was that it had gone.

CHAPTER 8

The copper came into the cell and thrust a mug of tea into my hand.

'Whit am I in for?' I asked.

'Are you no' the drunk and disorderly?'

'How should I know?'

'You must be. There wis only one admittance last night as far as I ken.'

I nodded in miserable acceptance and drank the tea, unable to remember anything that had happened the previous night after Craig and company had left me, apart from losing my wages.

'Ye didny find ma pay poke lyin' aboot?' I asked.

'Lyin' aboot where?'

I shrugged. 'I lost it, but it doesny matter.'

'We gathered last night ye'd lost it. By the noise ye were makin' it seemed tae matter then.'

'Is there nothin' tae eat?' I asked. 'I prefer tae eat when I'm drinkin' tea.'

'You've got a hope at this time in the mornin'. It's only five o'clock. Ye're lucky tae get tea.'

'When dae I get oot?'

'It's hard tae say. As far as I ken ye've been recommended for hospital treatment.'

'Hey, wait a minute,' I said, aghast, 'there's nothin' wrang wi' me, apart frae a hangover.'

'According to your record,' stated the copper, 'this is yer tenth time picked up drunk in the past six months.'

'Ye've got the wrang man,' I said. 'It's ma first time in this jail. I've only been a few weeks in the district. Ye'd better check the other cells.'

He said, standing with his hands on his hips like a big sweetie wife, 'Surprisin' as it might seem tae you, ye're the only drunk and disorderly in here, so there's nae mistake.'

I stood up and pointed to my face, placing it close to his. 'Tell me,' I said, 'have ye seen this particular set o' features afore?'

'I believe I have.'

'Ye're a bloody liar,' I said, 'and furthermore I want a lawyer.'

'Wid that by ony chance be a criminal one?' he said, heaving with suppressed laughter.

'I'm tellin' ye,' I said desperately, 'ye've got the wrang man.'

'I shouldny be in here,' I told the guy in the bed next to me in the hospital ward. 'It's a case of mistaken identity.'

He looked at me blankly, then removed a set of earphones which had escaped my attention. I repeated the information.

'Where should ye be, then?' he asked.

'No' in here. I only had a few drinks.'

'They a' say that. On the ither haun', ye could be one o' the weirdos or one o' the cracked up shots. It's no' a' alcies in here.'

He put the headphones on again, and closed his eyes as he leaned back on the pillow. He looked peaceful and happy. A male nurse appeared at the side of my bed and handed me three different coloured pills. He ordered me to swallow them immediately.

'I shouldny be in here,' I informed him. 'Somebody's made a mistake.'

'Yer mother, nae doubt.'

He winked at me and moved over to the guy with the earphones. 'Wake up, Charlie, and take yer pills, pet.'

Charlie opened his eyes, groaned and removed the earphones. 'These pills make me constipated. I huvny shit for three days.'

'At that rate,' said the nurse, wagging his finger, 'we'll have to gie ye an enema, won't we?'

'Jist gie me the pills,' said Charlie.

Afterwards I swung my legs over the bed, surprised to see I was wearing green pyjama trousers to match the green pyjama top, which I had thought was a shirt.

'Ye're no' supposed tae get up on yer first day,' said Charlie.

I explained that I was leaving straight away, but before I could take a step the male nurse along with a taller, broader male nurse approached me hastily and threw me back on the bed, then thrust me under the blankets and tucked me in very determinedly.

'Be good,' said the tall, broad nurse, flexing his muscles a bit, 'or we'll need to gie ye a wee jag tae calm ye doon.'

In a quiet and sensible way I explained that my presence here was a blunder on the part of the law, which I was prepared to overlook if they fetched me my gear and released me. Otherwise it wasn't improbable that I would be awarded a fair amount of compensation for wrongful detention. 'It happens a lot nooadays,' I told them. They shook their heads and surveyed me with sympathy, especially the one who had given me the pills.

'We'll see aboot this, pet,' he said.

Smartly and in step they marched out of the ward and returned in a short time. The big broad nurse carried a hypodermic needle.

'I've been around and I'm tellin' ye, man, there's a lot worse places than this,' Charlie was saying on what I gathered was my second day in the ward. I had been doped up for so long it was hard to tell.

'Free meals and a good bed,' he added wryly. 'Whit mair dae ye want?'

He was a good-looking guy, probably in his thirties, despite his grey side-locks.

'There's a few things I could mention,' I said. 'Like fags and a bottle o' whisky.'

He threw me over a packet of Embassy Regal. 'Ye can smoke as much as ye can afford. As for drink, well, it can be smuggled in if ye've got contacts, but I'm tellin' ye, man, they gie ye a particular kind o' pill afore ye go tae sleep which has the same effect as a stiff drink o' liquor. It's really some buzz.'

'I can hardly wait for it,' I said.

'So,' he continued, 'ye might as well dae whit they tell ye and take these vitamin pills on yer locker. It pays in the long run.'

I stuck the pills in my mouth and swallowed them with a glass of tepid water.

'It's like swallowin' golf balls.'

'Think yersel' lucky ye're no' gettin' the shock treatment.'

I became indignant. 'Lucky!' I said. 'When I shouldny be in here.'

'The first time I came here I got it for kickin' up a rumpus,' said Charlie.

'Maybe ye deserved it.'

'It's no' whit ye deserve. It's whit they think ye deserve. I learned the hard way tae be docile. Ye get on fine in here if ye're docile, so take ma advice and – '

'I know,' I said, 'dae whit they tell ye.'

I rested my head back on the iron rails of the bed head and watched a wee guy shuffle along the ward, trailing the cord of his dressing gown behind him like a tail as he peered at the floor.

'Whit's he daein'?' I asked. 'Lookin' for fag-ends?'

'Aye, it's force o' habit. He used tae search the railway station for fag-ends and onythin' else he could find.'

'Is that whit he's in for? It doesny seem much.'

'Aye, it doesny,' said Charlie. 'At one time the porters didny bother wi' him, but that wis afore the station wis modernised. Efter that he didny fit in wi' the new image. When the passengers signed a petition to get him removed because he smelled bad, he wis shoved in here temporary, for observation, they said. Then he really went bonkers, so he stays here a' the time. He's better aff noo, if ye ask me.'

'I think you're bonkers as well if ye like this looney bin. First opportunity I'm off, with or withoot ma gear.'

'Watch it,' said Charlie. 'Here comes Maurice. Act cool.'

Maurice, who was the coquettish male nurse, asked me how I felt.

'Great,' I said. 'There's nothin' wrang wi' me. It's a shame to take up a bed when some poor bastard's likely needin' it.'

'Relax and enjoy yersel',' said Maurice as he lifted my wrist and pressed it with his thumb.

'Just as I thought,' he said. 'Yer pulse is too rapid. Ye've got an anxiety problem.'

In panic I backed away when he tried to shove a thermometer under my oxter. It fell on the floor. Breathing heavily, he picked it up and studied it with a frown.

'Is it broke?' Charlie asked anxiously.

'Luckily it's no',' said Maurice, and placed it in his top pocket.

He regarded me sternly, then asked Charlie if I had shown any previous signs of violence.

Charlie said, 'Usually he's as quiet as a budgie.'

I sank further down the pillow while Maurice continued to study me.

'We'll see,' he said ominously, and moved off to the next bed, occupied by an old guy who slept most of the time. He didn't leave me a single pill.

'Dae ye think I'll get the shock treatment?' I asked Charlie, now engrossed in a paperback called *Rustlers' Ransom*.

'I warned ye,' he said, keeping his eyes fixed on the page.

I stared up at the ceiling, thinking that Maurice could be right about my rapid pulse and anxiety problem. My heart was pounding and I felt anxious, but when he returned to the ward later he didn't even look in my direction. He simply clapped his hands and told us all to sit up and look cheerful. The visitors had arrived.

'That's us trapped in bed for a whole bloody hour,' said Charlie.

'Dae ye no' get ony visitors then?' I asked.

'Are you kiddin'?' he sounded as if the very idea of a visitor would make him sick.

'It would pass the time,' I said, but I was content to be in the same boat as Charlie.

At the last minute someone shouted from the other side 'Jackie's shit hissel',' whereupon Maurice and the tall, broad male nurse, arrayed with screens and a bedpan, charged down the ward in a ferocious manner. When the visitors entered the ward, dubious expressions on their faces, we were all holding our noses. Then Charlie picked up his paperback and I pulled the cover half over my face to suggest extreme debility to anyone looking in my direction. I closed my eyes and might have dozed off if someone hadn't scraped a chair near at hand. I opened my eyes a fraction to see Nancy sitting at my bedside regarding me sadly, her fresh cut grass perfume wafting up my nostrils. My first sensation was joy, then embarrassment.

'You shouldny have came,' I said stiffly.

She handed me a box of fruit jellies and said with resentment as she stared at me, 'I didn't know you were allowed to smoke.'

I sat up slowly and gave her a cautious glance, thinking that every time I saw her she always looked better than before. 'How did ye find me?' I asked.

'It's a long story.' She went on to say she had found out where I was through Jimmy, who had found out through the lodger called Dad, who said that he'd been delivering newspapers to the hospital and had seem me being escorted into the ward by the male nurses. The thought crossed my mind that this was no coincidence and that my movements were being noted, but since my head was as fuzzy as a ball of wool I couldn't hold on to the notion. It was much easier to concentrate on Nancy's green eyes with the yellow flecks, and the way the bridge of her nose was covered in freckles that I hadn't seen before.

'Gie's a kiss,' I said.

She leaned over and barely touched my lips.

'Why are you in here?' she asked.

'I'm no' sure. I must have taken a blackoot.'

'What caused it?'

'I'm no' sure.'

We both fell silent. I began to rummage among the fruit jellies. I offered her one. She took the box and handed it over to Charlie, still absorbed in his paperback. He looked startled and shook his head.

'He's on a diet,' I explained.

She placed the fruit jellies on top of the locker and we fell silent again. When she began fiddling with her watchstrap I asked her if she wanted to leave. She said of course not and asked me if I wanted her to leave. I said why did she have to twist everything. I could hear Charlie thrashing around in his bed like a fish on the rocks.

'I've been told you've lost your job,' she said.

'Don't worry. I'll get anither.'

At this point Charlie threw the paperback down on the cover, leapt from his bed and ran down the ward wearing only a pair of pants under the pyjama top. His legs were surprisingly thin.

'What's wrong with him?' asked Nancy.

'I think it's his gall bladder.'

'That's funny,' she said, looking at me suspiciously. 'I was told this was a psychiatric ward.'

'That, amongst other things,' I said vaguely, looking towards the exit and expecting to see Charlie being escorted back any minute with his feet scarcely touching the ground.

'They said you had drink-related problems.'

'Who said?'

'Is it true?'

I sat up straight and confronted her fierce expression. 'I have ither problems as well. Did they tell ye that?'

Then Maurice the male nurse came over and stared at Charlie's empty bed as though he couldn't believe his eyes. He looked at me and said, 'Are ye all right, pet?' without making any reference to Charlie.

'Sure,' I said, and added, 'I think Charlie's away for a – ' I was going to say piss, but hesitated because Nancy hated the word.

'Not to worry,' said Maurice, hurrying off. I hoped that Charlie hadn't blotted his record of docility.

'I'm sorry,' said Nancy, as if chastened by the arrival of the male nurse. 'I can see you are not well.'

I said, 'I might feel better if you came and sat on the edge o' the bed so's I can get a whiff o' yer perfume.'

Shyly she sat on the edge of the bed. We held hands and were very friendly for the remainder of the visit.

Before she left she said, 'I almost forgot about this message I was to give you from Jimmy.' She fumbled in her bag saying, 'I've got it written down somewhere.'

She handed me a scrap of paper. The writing in pencil was

not very clear, but I managed to make out the words 'Dad says be prepared for a fresh start. He will contact you at the lodgings.' Under this was the separate scribble of 'A' the best, Jimmy.'

What impressed me most about this note was that there was no mention of any money found, such as my lost wages.

Without any explanation I was discharged two days later. Before I departed Maurice took my blood pressure. 'Just a formality, pet,' he said as he tightened the band on my arm. 'Better to be safe than sorry.'

'Aren't you the lucky one,' said Charlie in a listless way. He was lying flat on his back without a pillow. There were purple rings round his eyes. He looked dazed. It was the first time I had seen him since Nancy's visit.

'Whit happened tae him?' I asked Maurice, who merely shook his head and put a finger to his lips. I shook Charlie's hand before I left and said to him in a jovial manner that I hoped to see him in Donavan's pub the following Friday. This was a pub which he had mentioned frequently in his discourses on the subject of drinking places.

'You bet,' he said in a slurred voice and closed his eyes.

Maurice slapped me playfully on the shoulder. 'Charlie's a good boy,' he said. 'No' like some I could mention.'

CHAPTER 9

I was picking up my hold-all in the bedroom of the lodging house when Danny crept up behind me. 'Whit are ye daein'?' he asked.

'Collectin' ma gear.'

He grabbed the handle. 'Ye don't collect nothin' until ye pay whit ye owe.'

I shoved his hand aside. 'I'll send the money when I can. I'm skint.'

He grabbed the handle again and I shoved him on to the bed, where he lay reclining on one elbow. When I left the room he shouted on his father, who was waiting at the bottom of the stairs with his arms folded across his chest like something from Stonehenge.

'Take his bag aff him,' shouted Danny from above. 'He owes us money.'

'Whit's in it,' said his father, 'gold?'

'Look,' I said, 'I'm startin' anither site on Monday. I'll send ye the money when I get a wage. I canny dae any better than that.'

'Confiscate his possessions,' said Danny, his breath now heavy on my neck.

'Possessions?' I laughed.

His father told Danny to be quiet and asked me what was in the hold-all.

'Holey socks and semmits. Dae ye want a look?'

When I made to unzip it he gestured for me to leave it alone, saying, 'I don't want tae see yer dirty rags, so long as ye've nane o' ma sheets or towels.'

I assured him that I hadn't and asked him to let me past since I had to catch a bus.

'It so happens yer digs have been paid,' he growled.

'Naebody telt me that,' said Danny, shoving his face between me and his father.

As casually as I could I said, 'I suppose it would be auld Dad that paid it. He mentioned something to that effect when I saw him last and I would gie him the money later – '

'Who said it wis Dad?' Danny's father interrupted.

'Who wis it then?'

'There wis an envelope shoved under ma door wi' money in it for yer digs as indicated in the letter, but there wis nae signature.'

To quell his suspicious stare I said, 'I think I know who it wis.' Recalling Dad's cryptic message that I should be prepared for a fresh start, I asked, 'Wis there nothin' else mentioned in the letter?'

'Not a thing, but if ye don't believe me – ' he began to say.

'Sure, I believe you,' I said quickly. I was actually more concerned about making a rapid exit from their company than wondering who the benefactor was. I was sure it was Colin Craig, but I had lost interest in his plans. Besides, Nancy was waiting outside.

'I should have been telt aboot this,' said Danny.

'You get through tae the kitchen and attend tae yer chores,' his father said, taking a step towards him. Danny moved quickly out of the lobby with his father following. I paused only long enough to hear the sound of Danny's raised voice, then the noise of something banging, like a pot falling on the floor.

I walked outside, blinking in the sunshine, to where Nancy was leaning against the railings surrounding the grass verge in front of the terraces. She linked her arm through mine in a proprietory manner, as though we were married. She had taken a day off from the office when she learned I had been released from the hospital.

'There was no trouble then?' she said, giving my shabby hold-all a critical glance.

'Why should there be?'

I told her I would have to pay a visit to the labour exchange.

'For another job?'

'For broo money, if I can get it.'

I explained brutally that there was no chance of me getting a job, and not much either of getting money. She might as well take note of the fact that I was a pauper.

'Don't worry,' she said gripping my arm, 'I'll get you a room with my aunt. She's very nice.'

'I canny dae that,' I said.

But she dismissed this with a laugh. 'Of course you can, and the good thing about it is that I can come to your room whenever I want.'

It sounded fine, especially the bit about her coming to the room, but the sudden release from the mental ward had left me depressed. I was crazy about this classy dame, who surprisingly hadn't complained too much about all the trouble I had given her, yet all I wanted at this moment was a pint of beer in a quiet bar where the ashtrays were still fresh from the morning's rub.

'Won't you like that?' She asked.

'Sure,' I said. 'It's the money situation that bothers me.'

'But you'll get some from the labour exchange, surely. No one starves nowadays.'

'I keep forgettin' that.' I gave her a sidelong glance and asked, 'Ye widny like tae buy me a pint o' beer? I've got a terrible thirst. The hospital makes ye awful dehydrated.'

She released my arm, saying, 'You'd better get it straight that from now on it's either me or the pub.'

'Whit kind o' choice is that?' I said meekly, and pulled her arm back through mine. 'Ye know I wis only jokin'.'

There were no jobs to be had in the broo, but I had the promise of a giro from the female clerk amounting to twenty-five pounds plus dig money, which was still to be assessed. I felt like shaking her hand when she informed me that I would get it through the post first thing in the morning.

'I suppose it's better than nothing,' said Nancy, her brow furrowed as though she had expected more.

'So,' I said, 'could ye lend me some money for the digs?'

'Any friend of my niece is a friend of mine,' said the aunt. She was a fat lady with plump smiling cheeks who explained that the room would be twelve pounds a week, including breakfast, and she did not require the money in advance. 'You have an honest face,' she said.

The room she showed us was cosily cluttered with pictures and ornaments and bits of furniture arranged round a high bed which looked as bouncy as a trampoline. There were silver framed photos jammed together on a table by the fire-place and the carpet was the heavy pile type that you sink into. I was afraid to move in case I marked it with my boots or knocked an ornament over with my elbows. I nodded to register approval, though inwardly feeling ill at ease under her fond gaze.

'I'll make you a bite to eat,' she said as I placed my bag gingerly on the bed. I fingered the tenner borrowed from Nancy which her aunt had not required in advance. 'We're jist gaun for a meal.'

Nancy raised her eyebrows in surprise.

'It's ma birthday,' I said.

'Why didn't you tell me?' said Nancy.

'I would have made you something special,' said the aunt.

'There's nae problem,' I said, backing towards the door.

On the way out the aunt followed us to the doorstep and expressed the hope that we would enjoy ourselves, adding wistfully, 'You're only young once.' I felt especially guilty about this, since I had been wondering how I was going to retrieve my bag from her room.

The licensed restaurant where we sat studying the menu wasn't my idea of a place to enjoy yourself, with its oak panelling and aspidistra plants, and most of all it's steep prices.

'I thought we'd go somewhere special, since its your birthday,' said Nancy.

'It's the prices – ' I began.

'Don't worry,' she said, patting my knee under the table. 'It's my treat.'

Shamefaced, I admitted that it wasn't my birthday and that I had said this to get out of her aunt's house, because, though I thought her aunt was a very nice lady and the room comfortable, the fact was that the place gave me claustrophobia, something I was prone to in certain premises, the reasons for which were unaccountable.

'I see,' she said, looking downcast.

'Cheer up,' I said, returning the pat on the knee, 'we'll kid on it's ma birthday. I'm bound to have one some time.'

The chicken that we ordered was a problem. It slid off the plate when I stuck in the fork, marking the tablecloth. I picked it up with my fingers and told Nancy that this was how the upper crust ate their food, as far as I knew. 'The easiest way possible,' I said with a laugh.

Her eyes were fixed on her plate as she cut her own chicken delicately.

She said, 'There's a napkin on the table if you want to wipe your hands.'

'Thanks,' I said.

'And mouth,' she added.

The waitress returned to ask if we wished for a sweet.

'I didn't even wish for the chicken,' I said, attempting to joke.

'I know what you mean,' she said. 'Chicken can be dodgy at times. You've got to be in the mood for it. But I can definitely recommend the sweet.'

'Well – ' I began, looking at Nancy.

'I don't think we'll bother.'

Before she could take out her purse I paid for the meal with the tenner in my pocket and told the waitress to keep the change. 'It's too much,' she said, but I waved this aside. It was fine to act rich for once.

'Last of the big spenders,' said Nancy when we were outside.

I shrugged as I smiled full into her face. 'I must say I enjoyed that chicken'.

'No you didn't,' she said. 'But since it's your birthday I'll buy a drink. I know you'll like that.'

'But it's no' ma birthday.'

'You're bound to have one some time.'

We walked along the street arm in arm and stopped outside a close tiled in the corporation style of white with blue borders, though the tiles were cracked. The place was very quiet.

'Do ye think I could get a wee smooch in here to be gaun on wi'?' I asked.

She nodded shyly and I lead her by the hand up to the first landing. We made love in the corner of this landing in such a still and furtive way that it would have been hard to prove, apart from our painful and heavy breathing. But there's always someone who can see through a situation. A female voice called from above, 'If ye don't get away frae this decent close I'll get the polis.'

Giggling but embarrassed we scurried down the stairs. Outside, Nancy said, her face flushed, 'Where should we go for a drink? It's your choice.'

I couldn't think where to go that would be suitable. I knew hardly any pubs apart from The Open Door, which was about the worst place to take any dame. Then I thought, why not? It was my choice, but more important it was an opportunity to see McLerie and enquire about the fresh start, if there was such a thing. Anyway, there was no harm in trying.

'I know a place,' I said. 'It's no' very nice, but there's a guy goes there who's startin' up his ain business. There's maybe a post in it for me.'

'It's as good a reason as any,' said Nancy, linking my arm.

'This place is a ruin,' she said when we stood facing The Open Door.

'I'll admit it's a mess, but it's better inside.' I shoved the door but it refused to budge.

'It's definitely closed,' said Nancy.

'I think the hinges are stiff.'

I gave it some heavy kicks and it swung open with the lock dangling.

'You shouldn't have done that,' said Nancy. 'The place was locked.'

'Maybe,' I said vaguely and walked straight through into the poky drinking quarters. There was no one about and the air was chilled as if there had been no one about for some time. Most of the glasses were gone apart from a few extremely dulled ones on the shelves standing alongside the Red Hackle bottles, which turned out to be empty.

'This place is disgusting,' said Nancy.

'Ye're right, but we might as well look around while we're here.'

Whistling to convey that I wasn't daunted by all this, I entered the back room with Nancy close at my heels. The cupboard door swung open. The shelves inside were bare, apart from an old newspaper lying on the top one. I brought it out to have a look at the date. It might give me a clue as to when Craig and his pals were last here. Then something scuttled under the sink with the verdigris tap and Nancy gave a shriek.

'It's only a moose or a rat,' I said, throwing down the paper. She now moaned with fear. On my knees, I peered into the corner, but the rodent had vanished. All I found was a cloth stiff with age next to a bottle, which I took out and discovered to be half full of gin, according to the label.

'Look,' I said, holding it up as though I'd won a prize.

Nancy wrinkled her nose. 'What is it? Weedkiller?'

'I'll soon find oot.'

I fetched two tumblers from the bar and washed them under the verdigris tap. 'Will ye be wantin' some if it's gin?' I asked her.

'I might, if there's orange.'

I gave a mock sigh of despair and told her, after taking a deep sniff at the contents of the bottle, that it was gin, but she would have to take it with water as there was no orange.

She smiled. 'Whatever you say.'

'There's one thing aboot this pub,' I said, 'it's quiet enough.'

'And the drink's cheap, too.'

I spread out the newspaper to cover the dust on the table and poured the drink, adding a suitable amount of water. We sat facing each other sombrely as we sipped the gin. I decided I would be a fool not to take the room with Nancy's aunt. It looked as though the birds here had flown the coop. There was no point in trying to chase shadows.

'The only thing missing now,' said Nancy, as though she could read my mind, 'is the man with the job.'

'Ye canny have everythin'.

I was about to kiss her and tell her that my claustrophobia might not be as bad as I thought and that I was going to take her aunt's room, when I spilled some gin on top of the news paper. As I glanced at the mark a headline caught my eye. It read: LIFE AS NATURE INTENDED. But what really riveted me was the photograph of the guy underneath called Major A.R. Burns, who was the living spit of Colin Craig, even to the handlebar moustache. I hurriedly read the article. It stated that this Major Burns was the leader of a group called Lifeline, who intended to live in the northern wilderness as close to nature as they could. 'Free from the shackles of civilisation' was the quote. I pondered on this for a while and decided that the guy's resemblance to Craig was no coincidence; neither were the initials A.R.B. that I had noticed on Craig's wallet on the day of the peace festival. It was Craig. It all fitted: the business he was about to start, the abandoned pub, and now the group called Lifeline. I could have been part of it if I had waited on at the lodgings for Dad's message.

'What's the matter?' Nancy asked.

I showed her the paper, indicating the article and the photograph. 'That's the guy who wis gaun tae gie me a job,' I said.

'He looks nice, like someone I've seen somewhere.'

'I widny be surprised if he's part o' some spy ring.'

'You'd take a job with a spy ring?' she said, surprised.

'If the money's good enough.'

I was joking about the spy ring, but I suspected something shady was going on with Dad, McLerie and Craig. I'd have been a fool not to, considering all that had happened since I'd encountered Craig. For instance, getting arrested for only being drunk and tossed into a local institution, then released without explanation as if I was being held pending enquiries. Then Danny had let slip about the police watching the digs. Who were they watching, me or Dad, or just anyone? Yet at the same time I was interested. It was as though the article had been written solely for me. Hadn't Craig said that my life was more likely to alter if I did something about it, rather than waiting passively for something to happen? Here was the challenge.

'Actually,' I said to Nancy, 'this guy's a mate o' mine. He's a real gentleman. It's a great pity I didny catch him afore he left the district.'

'I'm surprised he chose to drink in here if he's such a gentleman,' said Nancy, looking around disdainfully.

'It wis jist a meetin' place. Folk like him don't need tae be seen in fancy places.'

I don't know why I was trying to convince Nancy how great the man was when the signs about this were doubtful.

There was a long pause before she said, 'Perhaps you should go to that place and see him, if it means so much.'

'Did I say it meant so much?'

She didn't answer. She merely took a sip of her gin, then stared at her glass.

'Anyway,' I said, 'dae ye think I'd want tae leave you?'

'And there's my aunt's room,' she pointed out.

'I know.'

We fell silent, then we both spoke at the same time. We began to laugh.

'Whit were ye gaun tae say?' I asked.

'I suppose you can't give up the chance so easily,' said Nancy.

'Whit chance?'

'I thought you said this man had work for you?'

'That's true,' I said. I wondered now if it was true. I tried to remember Craig's exact words about getting me fixed up. I said to Nancy, 'I could definitely get a job. So dae ye think I should go up tae that place – ' I peered into the newspaper – 'Langholm Valley, that's whit it's called.'

'How would you get there?' asked Nancy, sadly.

'Hitch-hike, I suppose.'

I lapsed into silence again while I calculated how far I would get on the twenty-five pounds giro plus the dig money to be sent care of Nancy's aunt, less the ten pounds I owed Nancy.

'If you go,' said Nancy, 'I might never see you again.'

'Of course you will,' I said. 'Dae ye think I'd be gone forever?'

'And if there's no job . . . what if it's a wild goose chase?'

I smiled. 'A wild goose chase? I like the sound o' chasin' the wild geese.' I became serious. 'I honestly don't know whit I'd dae if there's nae job.'

'There you are,' she said. 'You don't know what would happen, so I'd likely not see you again.'

'Anyway, I've changed ma mind. I'm no' gaun.'

I poured out the last of the gin into each of our glasses and stared ahead morosely. What a fool I was to talk about going anywhere in the impoverished state I was in. Then she said, suddenly excited, 'Do you know, I've got a brilliant idea?'

'Whit's that?'

'I could take my holidays now from the office and come with you.' I stared at her open-mouthed as she continued. 'It could be a camping holiday, and at the same time we could travel up to that place you mentioned.'

'Langholm Valley.'

'That's right. I know where I could borrow a tent and sleeping bags as well as a stove and pots. We would be killing two birds with the one stone, and I've always wanted to go camping.'

'But,' I said, taken aback now that a definite decision was being made, 'ye know whit they say?'

'What?' she asked, slightly breathless.

'He travels fastest who travels alone.'

She shook her head impatiently and went on to tell me of the arrangements she would have to make with her boss in the office, her parents and her aunt, and some other relatives she'd never mentioned before. I felt vaguely uneasy, but glad in a way it was all being settled for me.

CHAPTER 10

We stepped down from the train, Nancy and I, at the end of the line, at a place called Grinstone, along with another solitary passenger who shot through the barrier while we fumbled for our tickets. The air was damp and cold, like the look on the collector's face when he let us pass.

We dumped our rucksacks on a wooden bench and I muttered under my breath, 'Welcome to sunny Grinstone,' feeling depressed.

'I wonder where the ladies' room is,' said Nancy.

'Ask the collector.' When we looked round he had vanished.

'Don't tell me it's raining,' said Nancy, mystified and holding out her hand.

'It's wet whatever it is,' I said, studying my damp packet of fags.

Nancy said she was hungry and began to loosen the belt of her rucksack. I told her to leave it meanwhile, since the food was at the bottom. 'Yes, sir,' she said, with narrowed eyes.

I told her if she was going to be awkward there was no point in going on, even though we had just newly arrived.

Her lips quivered. 'Do you want me to go back?'

'I'm only askin' ye tae be reasonable.'

'I am being reasonable. I'm hungry. What's unreasonable about that?'

To placate her I said that we would buy pies and ginger when we reached the first shop.

We came to a church, a school, and a row of cottages.

'Where's the shop?'

I didn't answer. I was looking for a pub or a hotel.

'What's that?' said Nancy as we passed what seemed to be a cottage with a notice in the window, which on closer inspection read: 'Licensed to sell Beer and Spirits'. I dumped my baggage on the pavement and told Nancy to wait while I investigated. I tripped down three stairs into a dim room with low rafters, which appears to be the style of the northern drinking dens. The barman, who was polishing the counter, looked up startled. Two old guys came out from the shadows.

'Is it OK to bring the girlfriend in here?' I asked.

'Why not,' said the barman. He was the broad and burly type, like the proverbial village blacksmith. The old guys nodded approvingly.

'Meanwhile, I'll have a pint,' I said.

I enquired if there was a bus that went anywhere near a place called Langholm Valley. He informed me that there was no bus that went near anywhere. One of the guys said, 'Farlane McFarlane might take you as far as the Auchenachen

Inn, which is about half way, but he'll be doing his milk round at present and will not be back for maybe two hours.'

'Half way is better than nothin',' I said. 'Where can I reach him?'

'His house is the last one in the street with the milk-for-sale notice in the window.'

Nancy entered, looking agitated. The barman's face lit up and the old guys moved in closer. She informed me in a loud voice that she had decided to go back home on the next train.

'How's that?' I asked, aware of the old guys tutting and the barman leaning over his counter with arms folded.

'You left me alone in a strange place while you went drinking.'

'You knew I wisny far away.'

'I felt such a fool standing on the pavement with two rucksacks.'

'Where are the rucksacks?'

'On the pavement, where I left them.'

'For Christ's sake,' I said, 'they'll get stolen.'

'Don't worry,' said the barman who was looking to and fro from me to Nancy, 'there's no demand here for rucksacks.'

'And I'm absolutely starving,' said Nancy, catching her breath pathetically.

'Now, now,' said the barman in sympathy, 'I can let you have tea and sandwiches if it so pleases you.'

She clapped her hands in a childish way. 'That would be wonderful.'

The old guys smiled and nodded. I cleared my throat and asked if I could have some too.

We consumed thick beef sandwiches under the speculative gaze of the old guys and the barman, who had tossed his duster aside to concentrate his attention on Nancy. She munched her bread and drank her lager apparently unaware of the tension around her. A crumb stuck in my throat. I coughed and gasped for breath and thought I was going to die while they all watched. The panic subsided and I wiped the water from my eyes.

'Did you choke on something?' she asked.

I became unjustifiably angry. 'Hurry up,' I said, 'we're leavin'.'

The barman refused money for the meal. 'It was my pleasure,' he said, his eyes still on Nancy. She blushed and wiped her mouth, now looking embarrassed out of all proportion to his remark. I threw some silver down and brusquely told her to move. The old guys shrank back. One of them called, 'McFarlane should take you to the Auchenachen Inn with no bother. The owner is a fine figure of a woman and he always likes the excuse for a visit – that is, if he is not attending to his cows.'

McFarlane's house was easy to find, displaying the milk-for-sale notice in the window. His wife, a straw-haired woman as thin as a rake, told us that he wasn't home. She added, 'He's likely at the Auchenachen Inn visiting that black-haired besom Jessie Broden, so he could be there all day,' and slammed the door in our faces.

'We'll wait anyway,' I said to Nancy.

Two hours later we were bumping along a rough track in Farlane McFarlane's milk van, skirting close to a steep cliff. I had told this sandy-haired guy that we wanted to reach Langholm Valley, and explained that according to the newspapers a group of folk were about to develop the land in this area. Casually I asked if he had heard about it. He shook his head and said, 'Ach, the newspapers.' I kept quiet after that, since I didn't want to distract his attention from the abyss of rock falling away before us at every bend. Besides, Nancy's grip on my arm was painful.

'It's a bit rough,' McFarlane shouted above the rattle of his van, 'but it's a short cut. I don't like to leave the wife too long on her own.'

When we came to a main road he slowed down as long as it

takes to draw a breath, then he was off again like a rocket, but at least it was a less nerve-wracking journey. Soon we were drawing up outside the Auchenachen Inn. Against the backdrop of gloomy hills this solid white building with its latticed windows and patio surrounds looked like an optical illusion. The rusty motor lying adjacent to the pub was another incongruous touch. We had scarcely picked up our rucksacks from the back of McFarlane's milk van before he was away, the dust flying behind him. Maybe he had his cows to attend to.

The lounge inside was spacious, with pale plastic divans placed round glass-topped tables and scores of tumblers hanging from the roof. A dark-haired female was leaning over the bar reading a magazine – no doubt the dreaded Jessie Broden. She looked up startled when I coughed. She touched her throat.

'In the name o' God, where did you come from?'

I explained that Farlane McFarlane had dropped us off in his milk van.

'Isn't he the civil one,' she said.

'I was wonderin' – ' I began, looking around doubtfully. The room was empty apart from the three of us.

'We're open,' she said, 'if that's what you are wondering.' She added with a throaty chuckle, 'Come to think of it, we're always open.'

Although she was too plump and old for me, I could understand what McFarlane saw in her. The look in her eye alone was distracting.

Nancy whispered in my ear, 'Ask her if we're far from Langholm Valley.'

'Gie us a chance,' I said under my breath.

'I would say,' said Jessie Broden, 'it's about four hours to Langholm Valley by car, and four days by foot.' She added sympathetically, 'I suppose you'll be hiking it.'

'We might as well stop for a bit then,' I said, and turned to Nancy. 'We could get a drink and something to eat.'

Nancy said angrily, 'We've had that already.'

As though she hadn't heard this Jessie Broden said, 'At the moment I've only got some soup left over from yesterday, but it's always better the second day anyway.'

'It's much too hot for soup,' Nancy retorted, but the woman was out of the bar and calling for two platefuls.

We supped this at one of the glass-topped tables with red faces, on acount of the hot meal and the drawing of a naked woman in the depth of an ashtray lying between us which strongly resembled the hostess.

'I can't swallow any more of this,' said Nancy letting soup from her spoon trickle back to the plate.

'Right,' I said, and explained to Jessie Broden that we would have to leave if the journey was as far as she had indicated.

'You're not thinking of starting off already,' she said, and suggested that we should camp at the river nearby, adding, 'And you can come back later when the place is busy. Someone might give you a lift. Forbye that we'll be having a cheery sing-song.'

'I don't think so,' said Nancy, tossing her head as she walked out.

Jessie said consolingly, 'It's the heat. We're not used to it.'

'I didn't like the look of that woman,' said Nancy when we were erecting the tent. 'She looked as if she could eat you. I bet she's man mad.'

I ignored this statement and told her that she wasn't driving the pegs in hard enough.

'And she looks forty if she's a day,' Nancy went on.

I frowned at the sight of clothing spread over the grass. Already the place looked like a tinker's camp.

'Leave the pegs and get some water from that stream,' I said, pointing vaguely in its direction.

'Anything else?' she asked threateningly.

'Try and keep the place tidy.'

'I refuse to be ordered about like a servant,' she said.

'You've been bossing me about ever since we got off the train.'

'An' you've moaned every inch o' the way.'

'Another thing,' she said. 'You're always heading for pubs.'

'There's nothin' else tae head for. Besides, so far I've only had two pints of beer.'

'If you had your way it would be a lot more.'

I picked up the hammer she had flung on the ground and started to go over the loose pegs. She lifted up a pot and headed for the stream. After the pegs were fixed and all the articles were arranged neatly inside the tent, I sat cross-legged scanning the ridge of hills confronting me, where sheep moved slowly like lice on a shaved head. I wasn't exactly entranced, but I thought that in time I might get to like the view. At the moment it unnerved me. I wondered why Nancy was taking so long with the water. Possibly she was wandering about gathering wild flowers, which are only weeds. I've seen dames do this sometimes when I've been trying to sleep off the booze on a hillside in the warm weather. If they see you they panic because they think you're either a flasher or a rapist. It's not possible for them to think you're only wanting to sleep. You can't blame them, though, for being like this because it happens now and again. On their own they've no chance against some kinky guy. I guess that's why they can never be equal. They're too weak. Even a kinky dame is no match for a kinky guy. I became worried. Where the hell was Nancy? She had been in a reckless mood when she left. I jumped up and ran through the tough grass shouting her name. It echoed back to me eerily. I was dragging my legs towards the stream, weighed down with anxiety, when she sprang out from a bush holding up a bunch of heather.

'I was trying to get lucky,' she said.

I grabbed her shoulders. 'You stupid dame. I thought you wir a goner.'

'You mean you hoped I was.'

'Throw that stuff away, and come back tae the tent and I'll gie ye somethin' that's luckier.'

Afterwards when we sat outside the tent watching, as if bemused, two eggs boil inside a pot on top of the primus stove, I chanced to suggest that we take a jaunt over to the inn to celebrate.

'Celebrate what?' Her voice was edgy.

'Our first day and that?'

'I'm tired.'

'Jist for a wee while. We'll come back early.'

'Why is it,' she said sadly, 'that you're always wanting to enter a pub? Isn't it much nicer to stay here and see all this?'

'Sure,' I said, 'I think it's great, but it can get monotonous, especially when the sun goes doon.'

Her face became set. 'I'm not going, especially to see that woman ogling.'

'Whit dae ye mean – ogling?'

'You know what I mean. I suppose that's why you're going.'

'Christ's sake, I wis gaun for the sing-song. As you say, that woman's forty if she's a day. Dae ye think I'd fancy a dame o' forty?'

She turned away and scooped the eggs from the pot with a spoon. White blobs had burst through the shell. She placed them on the grass. Her face was tragic. 'I hate sing-songs,' she said.

'I think ye are a snob,' I said. 'Ye don't like anythin' except maybe staring at the scenery. When we leave this place we might no' see anyone for days. Whit's wrang wi' a singsong?'

In answer to this she stood up and tossed the eggs into the long grass, then crawled into the tent, pulling the flaps together behind her.

I stood at a corner of the bar swirling two inches of beer around my tumbler. The place was busy. On the way in I had passed a variety of vehicles, including Farlane McFarlane's milk van, but at this moment there was no sign of him. Hefty farmer types were holding up the counter. Their womenfolk sat at the glass-topped tables playing cards. They wore loose print dresses like the kind my mother buys from Oxfam, but their fingers glittered with diamonds.

A voice spoke in my ear, 'It's yerself, is it?' I turned to face Farlane McFarlane. He looked beyond me to where Jessie Broden was conversing with some guys. Their eyes were fixed on the neck of her low-cut dress.

'I was chust saying,' said McFarlane when she came over to serve him, 'that it's himself, the one I gave the lift to.'

'You mean,' she said, giving me a bold stare, 'the one who is camping with his wife.'

'She's no' ma wife,' I said.

She raised her eyebrows, 'Fancy.'

'I wouldn't mind a bit of camping myself,' said McFarlane, after he had ordered a pint for both of us, which I thought was decent of him, 'if I could find a nice wee woman to share the blankets with.'

'I'd have thought,' said Jessie, her elbow on the counter and her face close to his, 'that you'd be all played out milking your cows.'

McFarlane stated, 'Right enough. It's a terrible profession I have for putting thoughts into your head.' He stared at Jessie's chest over his tumbler.

She said, tapping my arm but addressing McFarlane, 'You'll be putting ideas into this lad's head.'

'He'll have all the ideas there already,' said McFarlane.

'No' me,' I said, feeling self-conscious.

Jessie shrugged and moved away to serve, her hips shaking like blancmange. Furtively McFarlane brought out a half bottle of whisky from his inside pocket. 'Be quick with your beer and I'll pour some of this in before she spots it.'

I thanked him sincerely and explained that I wouldn't be stopping long. 'It's the girlfriend,' I said, 'she's no' keen on the drink.'

'They never are,' he said. 'That's why we do so much of it.

If my wife kept a bottle in the sideboard at home it would save me the bother of leaving.' As Jessie wobbled past our line of vision he added, 'On the other hand, there's something to be said for the company.'

Jessie turned back to us to say, 'If that's you drinking from your own bottle, McFarlane, you'll be out quicker than you can say your name.'

'You wouldn't be doing that to a man who's on the brink of a divorce,' he said quickly.

'Divorce – on what grounds?'

'On the grounds that my wife has gone off her head and soon will be entering an asylum.' He openly splashed more whisky into our tumblers. 'I'll be in sole charge of the milk round, which is doing very nicely.'

Jessie's eyes widened. 'You don't say.'

'Is that true?' I asked when she had moved off again. 'That your wife is gaun tae the looney bin?'

McFarlane sighed. 'Unfortunately no'. Actually, I'm a desperate man, with her being as hard and plain as a plank of wood and three of my cows dying with what might be the foot and mouth. But so long as Jessie thinks my prospects are good I'll be all right for the night, if you know what I mean.'

I was annoyed by his lascivious expression. I thought he had no right to have it at his age, when there were better fish in the sea, such as myself – not that I fancied Jessie, but in my opinion she deserved better than McFarlane, even in a temporary way.

I said, 'And bein' the owner here would be a great chance.'

'Indeed so.'

At this stage the whisky must have inflamed my brain. I considered asking Jessie for a job as a barman or anything else that was needed. Apart from the occasional drink on the side, it might lead to better things, like becoming her business partner. I even visualised Nancy installed as a waitress and my mother in the kitchen baking scones, which goes to show how drunk I was even if I didn't feel it. My mother has never baked a scone in her life as far as I know. When Jessie came back and reached out for the empty tumblers I grabbed her wrist and asked her for a kiss. With her free hand she slapped me and told me to get going. The farmer types and their womenfolk, who had been squawking like their hens, went quiet and stared over. McFarlane broke the silence by saying in a loud and pompous voice, 'I'd advise you to clear off this minute, since we're not the kind of people who allow our women to be molested by strangers.'

'Well spoken, McFarlane,' shouted a florid-faced guy. 'Dae ye need a haun' wi' the rascal.'

I held up my hands as though somebody had pulled a gun on me, but it was only in placation. 'OK,' I said, 'there'll be nae trouble. I'm leavin',' and walked out backwards. Outside I sat on the step of the rusty motor with my head in my hands, wondering how to reach the tent. The sky was pitch black.

I awoke to face a grey dawn shining through the canvas and Nancy standing over me holding out a mug of tea. 'I've got everything packed,' she said, 'except the tent.'

I sat up shivering, with nothing to cover me and only the cold touch of the groundsheet under me. 'I think I've got the flu.'

Nancy said, 'Hurry up and get up. I want to undo the pegs.'

Like a sick dog I crawled outside on my hands and knees a minute before the tent collapsed. I said that I felt terrible. 'Get out of my way,' she said. 'I'll need to fold up the tent.' I sat helpless while she did so.

As we walked past the Auchenachen Inn, with Nancy in the lead, I stopped to stare at Farlane McFarlane's milk van standing alongside the old rusty motor. My eyes travelled up to a latticed window where a light still shone.

Nancy looked back. 'Are you expecting a wave?' she asked sarcastically.

‘No’ really,’ I said.

‘Hurry up, then. I want to get away from that inn before it opens.’

I caught up with her and began to feel better. The nip from the early morning frost was clearing my head. ‘I’m sorry aboot last night,’ I said.

‘We won’t talk about it,’ she said stiffly, but she let me kiss her on the cheek anyway.

‘Things could be worse,’ I said, thinking about Farlane McFarlane, with his wife as plain as a plank of wood and his fancy woman who was only crazy about his prospects, and him with his cows having what might be the foot and mouth.

CHAPTER 11

Our progress was slow after we left Grinstone, mainly because we had wasted time trying to thumb lifts from drivers who passed on blindly.

Nancy said, 'You'd be the same yourself if you had a car.'

'I wouldny pass anyone hikin' through this wilderness. They're jist pure bastards.'

The sun had come out in full blast. We were just about ready to drop when we came to a farm track with a notice pinned to a tree reading: 'Eggs for Sale'.

'Should we get some?' asked Nancy.

'If you like.' A blue Cortina zoomed by as we threw down

our rucksacks. 'We might have got a lift,' moaned Nancy, her face red and sweaty. I told her to sit beside me and rest against the rucksacks.

'People might see us,' she said. We sat so close to each other we were nearly welded together with the heat. I stopped her protests with a kiss and we hurriedly made love on the grass verge, whilst remaining alert for traffic.

'It was hardly worth it,' she said afterwards, lying on her back with her eyes screwed up at the sun.

'It's always worth it.'

'What about the eggs?'

'They would cook inside their shells. Jist leave them.'

We walked on for an hour too exhausted to speak. Finally Nancy said, 'Let's stop or I'll collapse.'

'It makes it worse if we stop a' the time.'

'I don't care. I can't go on.'

'Look,' I said, pointing to a circle of trees in the distance, 'we'll stop there.'

'But it's miles away, and all uphill.'

'After that it'll be downhill. We'll make some tea,' I promised.

We climbed up and down and through a field of thorns to reach the river. The good thing about this wilderness was there were plenty of rivers. Nancy picked her way through the nettles with furrowed brow. 'You always take the worst paths.'

We sat on the riverbank gazing serenely ahead, drinking tea from the flowered mugs provided by the aunt.

'The mountains are so peaceful,' she said.

'You mean hills.'

'Whatever they are, they're peaceful. I could stay here forever.'

She stretched out flat and put her arms behind her head. I hoped she wouldn't sleep. I wanted to reach a less desolate area. I moved over and peered into the side of the river.

'Come and see the shoals of young fish.'

'I can't be bothered.'

The words had scarcely left her lips when she jumped to her feet screaming, 'I've been bit. I've been bit. I'm being bit everywhere.'

I ran towards her and was immediately stung on the side of the neck.

'Clegs,' I yelled.

We ran through the thorns back up the hill, trailing our rucksacks behind us with the clegs hot on our trail. Strangely enough they faded away when we reached the road. A few tardy ones stuck to our arms, still gorging. 'Let them take their fill,' I said, 'otherwise they'll bite.'

'I've been bit everywhere as it is,' wailed Nancy. 'I think I'm going to die.'

Eventually we got rid of them and Nancy asked me what the symptoms of blood poisoning were.

'Don't worry,' I said, 'yer blood's too fresh to get poisoned.'

'Are you sure?' she asked, staring at me through puffy eyes. She had lumps all over her face.

'Sure I'm sure.' I felt her burning forehead. 'You'll be OK. The best thing to make sure is to start walking and get the blood circulating.'

'Just when we were so happy,' she said.

By the time we reached the ruins of an old cottage our wounds were less painful. Two youths, nattily dressed in white tee-shirts and khaki shorts, leaned against a broken piece of wall drinking Coke. The green nylon haversacks lying at their feet looked like a dream. They were both fair-haired, as if related, and one of them had a beard. He asked us if we had come far.

'Far enough.' I stared at his can hoping he would offer us some Coke, but he finished it off and threw it behind him. The other one asked us jokingly if we had caught the plague.

'We were attacked by clegs,' said Nancy. She held out her arms for inspection.

'That's a shame.'

'Absolutely rotten,' said the bearded one.

I wasn't impressed by their style and their polite accents, and I didn't miss their sly glances towards each other. I told them that we'd have to keep moving since we were in a hurry to reach a certain destination.

'Wait a minute,' said one of them. 'We've got ointment that's good for cleg bites.' He rummaged in his haversack and brought out a wee tube, which he handed over to Nancy.

'Thanks a million,' she said.

I noticed they watched her intently rubbing the stuff on her neck and arms.

'You're definitely good Samaritans,' she said.

The one with the beard nudged his pal and said, 'We always like to give a helping hand, don't we Frank?' The other one grinned and winked. I refused their ointment and told Nancy to get moving.

'Already?' she said, regarding me with annoyance. She had taken off her rucksack.

'Aye, already.'

'Don't go, darling,' said the one called Frank. 'Stay with us and have fun.' They both giggled unpleasantly. I was surprised at their gall and thought they must be having some kind of trip when they were so sure of themselves.

Nancy looked at them doubtfully, then said to me, 'We'll go then.'

When she lifted up her rucksack the bearded one took it off her saying, 'Don't go if you don't want to.' His eyes flickered towards me as he added, 'We'll take care of him, won't we Frank?'

They both took a step towards us. Frank raised his arm holding the Coke can. I got the impression it was still heavy with Coke and good for a hefty blow to the head. The only thing I could do was to make a run towards them, like a bull on the rampage, with my rucksack still on my back. Frank's Coke can went flying as I landed on top of him. The other one ran off. Nancy was shouting, 'Leave him alone!', to whom I wasn't sure, but she pulled the rucksack off my back. I rose to my feet taking Frank along with me, then I placed him against the broken wall and slapped the dust from his tee-shirt and shorts. They were not so natty any more. He was crying with rage. I beckoned on the bearded one standing some yards away to come and join us, but he shook his head.

'Whit did ye have tae dae that for?' I asked the Frank guy, who was now rubbing his eyes with his fist and making a right dirty mess of them.

'It was him,' he snivelled, pointing to his friend in the distance, 'he's always egging me on to do things.'

'That's a shame,' I said, as I emptied out the contents of their blissfully light haversacks lying against the wall. Inside there were only some lightweight groceries and a flimsy box, which could have been anything from dope to French letters. I didn't investigate. I jumped on them for a bit, then crushed the mess under my heel. 'Let this be a lesson,' I said as I departed.

'Filthy wee creeps,' said Nancy when I caught up with her.

'It's a' your fault.'

'My fault!'

'Ye should never throw yersel' intae a situation withoot thinkin'. Ye've always got tae be wary o' strangers in lonely places.'

'Why should I be when I've got you to protect me?' she said snappily.

'That's true, but I'm no' Superman. They might have been bigger and had weapons.'

For a while she was silent as we tramped on, then she said, 'Do you know what I think?'

'Whit?'

'I think you're an insufferable prig.'

It was late afternoon and we were standing on a cliff top. We gazed down into a span of water that stretched as far as the eye could see. We tossed off our rucksacks and lay flat on our stomachs in order to view it better. Big white waves were dashing against the rocks below us and everywhere there were seagulls – hundreds of them, rising and swooping and perching on ledges in the cliff. Their cries were sad and eerie.

'I wish there was a beach where we could sunbathe,' said Nancy.

'That would spoil everythin'. It's no' a holiday resort. It's a lonely, wild place. You could call it untamed. Look at these waves. They must be nearly ten feet high.'

'It gives me the shivers.'

I pointed to an area of shingle between the rocks. 'I bet there's a cave doon there and there's bound to be plenty o' seagulls' eggs.'

'I don't fancy seagulls' eggs.'

'That's because ye've never tasted them.'

'I don't want to taste seagulls' eggs. You'll slip and get killed. I'll be left here alone.'

'Don't be daft,' I said, and was over the cliff before she could protest. A few minutes later her voice drifted faintly on the air, then faded under the roar of the waves. Slowly I descended backwards, placing my feet into grooves in the rock. I was alarmed by the whish of seagulls' wings close to my head as they screamed at me, but for the sake of the challenge I forced myself downwards and reached the shingle, which was covered in ice-cold water. There is not much you can do when standing with wet feet on a patch of gravel with a circumference of about three yards facing an opening in the rock, other than enter it and advance a few steps. I found it difficult to continue since I appeared to have entered a black hole that smelled poisonous. I put out my hands to feel my way and touched something wet and scaly. Reason told me it was fungus or seaweed, but still I was shot through with a strong urge to retreat back to the shingle. I had remembered the tale of the legendary cannibal caveman Sonny Bean. I backed off in panic. Outside the seagulls perched on ledges followed me with their pebbly eyes. I scrambled past them expecting the thrust of their beaks any second, but they kept their heads better than I did. I could almost feel their scorn as I clumsily pulled myself upwards. I reached the top panting and breathless and threw myself down on the grass, exhausted.

'Where are the seagulls' eggs?' asked Nancy, the bottom of her jeans on a level with my face.

'Still in their nests.' Actually there wis nothin' much tae see doon there.'

'Didn't you hear me shouting about that warning over there?'

I raised my head to follow the direction of her finger pointing to a notice which read: DANGER – EARTH LIABLE TO SUBSIDENCE.

'How come I never seen that?'

'Because you never took the time to see anything. I tried to warn you. Didn't I say that you'd get killed?'

'But I never,' I said defiantly, trying to erase the thought of being buried alive under a ton of rock.

Nancy said, 'Now who's throwing himself into situations?'

'I always know whit I'm daein',' I replied.

We were on a long stretch of road, flanked on one side by flat grassland and on the other by a monotonous line of hills. The clouds were gathering and there was no sign of shelter. My back ached under the weight of the rucksack. Nancy was humming under her breath, but then her rucksack was lighter than mine and she'd had a good rest during the time I had climbed down the rocks.

'Looks like rain,' I said.

'We'd better put up the tent before it starts.'

'It's too boggy here. We'll have to keep goin'.'

'This bit looks dry enough,' she said, stamping on a grassy mound.

'It's too near the road.'

'Are you expecting a camping site somewhere?' she asked heavily.

I said that I wasn't but I didn't believe in camping in a

place without shelter where the tent would be flattened by a heavy downpour. She said that she was willing to take the risk since there appeared to be no end to the dismal view ahead, but if I wanted shelter there was something which looked like an old castle lying on the slope of the hill that she had been watching for the past ten minutes.

'Ye might have mentioned it sooner,' I said.

It was only the shell of a castle without a roof. Inside the circle of stone there was grass and sheep dung.

'At least it's shelter,' said Nancy.

I thought if the stone collapsed it would be oblivion, but it was pointless to worry about everything. Already spots of rain were falling.

'OK,' I said.

Soon we were huddled inside the tent. Sausages were sizzling in the frying pan on top of the primus. It was warm and cosy. The light from the lamp hanging on top of the tent pole shone on Nancy's face. It was unusually serene. I wanted to hug her, but I might have spoiled the effect.

Quietly I said, 'I wish we could stay here forever like this.'

'Like what?'

'You and me, snug as a bug frae the rain. Nothin' to worry aboot apart frae burnin' the sausages.'

'Don't be daft. I could think of nothing worse than to stay here forever,' she said, her face still serene.

CHAPTER 12

We might have passed the place altogether if a lorry hadn't slid out from an entrance hidden by a shrubbery. Being curious we wandered a few yards down a woodland path, where everything shimmered in the heat trapped within the trees. The birds were going crazy with their shrill songs. I thought I could feel some kind of magic here. I always feel this in woods or old estates. It's something to do with the smell of leaf mould.

'We could be trespassing,' said Nancy.

'We could be. I wish I had a knife so I could carve oor initials on a tree to mark that we were here.'

'What a funny notion.'

We moved along the path on tip-toe, though I don't know why. Our steps were soundless in the grass. We came to a big house, grimy with age but grand with its turreted roof and engraved doorway.

'It's definitely private property,' Nancy whispered.

'But it's empty.' I pointed to the blank windows, then to the sunken garden where flowers grew alongside weeds and tall grass, then to the rhododendron bushes.

'Let's go back,' she said.

Ignoring this, I went round to the rear of the house, which was cold in the shade and neglected looking. I peered through a window into what appeared to be a kitchen with a sink and cooking range. Two filled canvas bags rested against a wall. When Nancy asked me if there were signs of anybody about, I told her with a meaningful stare, 'No' for miles.'

'I hope not,' she said, smiling weakly.

We sank down in the long grass and made love slowly and expertly, as though we had been doing it for years.

Afterwards a thought occurred to me: 'Whit if ye get pregnant?'

'I'm on the pill,' she said.

I said, 'Thank goodness,' but my sentiment wasn't altogether genuine.

We walked to the other side of the building and came to what might have been a vegetable patch, though there were no vegetables that I could see, only rhubarb growing near a shed. I threw away my fag end and idly followed its direction with my eyes. It had landed near a boot protruding from the shed, scuffed, but with a modern plastic sole. I investigated to see if there was another one to match it and discovered a guy sitting on the floor of the shed with one leg stretched out and the other bent beneath him.

'I wis jist lookin' aboot,' I said. 'I thought the place was deserted.'

'That's a' richt.' He stood up and I saw he was roughly

dressed, which meant that his gear was worse than mine. 'So long as ye're no' wan o' them snoopers,' he added.

I gave him a fag and explained that I was hiking around the country with my girlfriend. At this point Nancy peered in the hut and asked what I was doing. When she saw the guy she quickly withdrew. He stubbed out the fag after taking only one draw and placed it behind his ear, then started to tie up a canvas bag, similar to the ones I had seen in the kitchen, with a piece of string.

'Scrap,' he explained.

'Scrap?' I repeated. 'Is there much o' it aboot?'

He gave me a direct look. His eyes were the blue shade you associate with sailors and other guys who are continually exposed to the elements. I decided he was one of the travelling folk, in other words a tinker.

He said, 'Sometimes ma brither and me gets lucky. Sometimes no'.'

'Wis that yer brither in the lorry?'

'Very probable.'

'I wouldny mind bein' in that line masel',' I said wistfully.

He said, 'It so happens this hoose wis a bit o' luck, bein' oot the road, for we've got tae watch, ye ken. If we're caught loadin' the stuff it's the jile, or a heavy fine at the least.'

Impulsively I asked, 'Ye're no' needin' an extra pair o' haunds.'

'We've got a' the haunds we need for we're a big family.' He gave me a stealthy look. 'We're the travellin' folk.'

I told him that although I was hiking with the girlfriend I was looking for work at the same time.

'Whit kind o' work?'

'Buildin' work. I'm a brickie.'

He shook his head. 'There's nae buildin' up here. Naethin' but sheep and heather, as ye can see for yersel'.'

I told him that I'd heard there was a place near at hand where a new project was starting up, mentioning the word Lifeline and what I'd read about it.

He looked puzzled. 'Never heard o' it.'

'It's bein' run by a guy called Major Burns. It wis in the newspapers.'

'I never read the newspapers,' he said quickly.

'Maybe the word's no' got roon' yet.' I added with a grin, 'So I'll be the first to get ma claim in.'

I then asked him if it was far to Langholm Valley.

'Christ man, ye're staunin' in the very spot, and there's naethin' happenin' here except for a couple o' fellas diggin' a ditch two miles back.'

I shrugged. 'Ach well, somethin's bound to turn up, even if it's only ma toes.'

He regarded me with sympathy. 'If ye hing oan until ma brither comes back he micht gie ye a day's work.'

'Don't worry. We'll manage. Anyway the girlfriend's in a hurry to get movin'.'

'Aye,' he said, peering outside the shed, 'she looks gey fed up.'

From over his shoulder I saw Nancy staring sullenly down in our direction. When I bade him farewell he told me that if we were to keep going we would come to a wild and stoney region which would be sore on the feet, so maybe the best thing to do was to turn back. He doubted if there was any project starting up anywhere near here. I said that we would go on anyway since the weather was good. He waved me off looking concerned.

'This is a terrible place,' said Nancy. We were striding it out along a road running through hills of black rock, lumps of which lay close to the trail.

'There's hardly any grass,' she went on.

'Don't worry. We've still got grub left.'

'I mean, it's all so barren. It's like a huge quarry.'

'Probably been like this since the Stone Age.'

'Stone Age is right.'

A cloud spread itself over the sun and a wind sprang up. We both shivered simultaneously.

'Ye'd better put yer jacket on,' I said.

'I can't be bothered undoing the rucksack. The sun will be out again any minute.'

'I wouldn't bank on it,' I said, looking up at the rock above. It wasn't so much black as a mixture of brown and dark green, mixed with the purple, prickly heather which I had come to detest. It grew everywhere, camouflaging quagmires and rabbit holes and other traps.

'Wid ye fancy a picnic up there?' I said to Nancy, pointing at the rock with a facetious smile on my face. She drew me a look so hard it was like a slap. I hurried ahead of her, tight-lipped. We walked in grim silence for half an hour and the sun still did not come out, nor was there any break in the terrain. I began to whistle a doleful air. Inwardly I was worried.

'What's that you're whistling?' called Nancy from behind me.

'A tune,' I said, and stopped to turn round.

'I know it's a tune,' she said, then burst into tears.

'It's no' as bad as that, surely?' I said, walking back and putting my arms round her.

'I don't want to go any further,' she said, her face pressed on my shoulder, soaking my shirt.

'I don't like this place masel',' I said. 'We'll have a wee rest then we'll go back. Tae hell wi' it.'

We had scarcely put our rucksacks down when a car drew up and stopped. The woman at the wheel asked, 'Do you want a lift? I'm going as far as Ornack.'

'That would be fine.' We climbed into the back seat, pulling our rucksacks behind us.

After some minutes the woman said, with her eyes on the road, 'I hate this part of the journey. It's so ugly.'

'Ye're right there, missus.'

She looked round at me and repeated the word 'missus' with a twist to her mouth. With her heavily-powdered face and blue-rinsed hair I wondered what I was supposed to call her. Nancy said quickly, 'I don't know what we would have done if you hadn't come along.'

'It would have been a pity to have missed Lornack,' said the woman. 'It's a fine town.'

I asked her if there was any work in Lornack.

'If you mean employment,' she said, with her eyes still on the road and giving us a view only of the back of her head, 'I'm afraid not.' She added, 'But even so, there are far too many unemployed people who don't try for anything. When I was young it was no better. I was forced to leave the district to get a position as a housemaid in London. That's what I had to do, but what can you expect when they get their money for nothing nowadays?'

We both stared stonily ahead for the remainder of the journey with no inclination to speak. She must have sensed our disapproval, for she dropped us off at a hotel near the edge of a loch explaining that she was going no further, then after that she drove straight on over the highway.

'Anyway, I'm glad to get away frae her,' I told Nancy, who was walking quickly past the hotel. She needn't have worried. I had spied the notice in the window which read TEMPERANCE HOTEL.

Eventually we arrived in the main street of Lornack, with its shops and cafés and windows full of souvenirs.

'I wish I could buy something to take back,' said Nancy, looking in at some knick-knacks.

'I don't know aboot somethin' tae take back,' I said, 'but ye can buy somethin' such as two fish suppers.'

While we were waiting for the fish to fry I purchased two packets of cigarettes. 'In case I run oot o' them when we get back tae the lonesome trail,' I explained.

She frowned. 'It's a pity you smoke. It costs such a lot.'

'Ye knew I smoked when ye first met me.'

'I know, but it's still a pity.'

Outside the café I could hardly wait to throw away the brown wrapper and bite into the crisp batter round the fish. 'This is terrific,' I said, panting to cool down the hot food in my mouth.

'Do you have to be such a litter lout?' she said, picking

the wrapper off the pavement and depositing it in a bin. I shrugged and continued to eat. I was finished long before her. She swallowed her food as if there was a lump in her throat. 'I'm not all that hungry,' she said when I looked at her enquiringly.

I asked a passer-by if there was a pub near at hand. 'The Locheil Bar is round the corner if you fancy a ceilidh,' he said.

'Let's go,' I said to Nancy, pretending not to notice her frown.

Inside the pub, which was noisy and overcrowded, we were asked to leave our rucksacks near the men's toilet and go into the lounge. Women weren't allowed to drink in the public bar.

'But that's discrimination,' said Nancy.

I shoved her through the door marked 'Lounge' saying, 'These are primitive parts. Don't argue.'

The clients, who were all fairly sunburnt, or maybe just red with the booze, squeezed up to make a place for us on the bench running along the length of the wall. Crushed against me was a stout woman who said that we were just in time for the McCann Brothers. 'They're smashin',' she stated. I asked Nancy if she preferred a vodka and orange.

'Prefer it to what?' she asked with dulled eyes.

The McCann Brothers, who were fiddlers, played lively tunes much appreciated by the clientele, who stamped their feet and clapped their hands to the beat. They all had drinks in front of them on the tables, which can doubtless make a difference to your capacity for appreciation.

'They're no' a bad group,' I said to Nancy. She nodded slightly, but remained withdrawn. I asked her what was wrong. She said that she had a headache. I was about to suggest leaving when the waiter arrived and took my order. It was no better after that because the music was loud and insistent on the eardrums and we were pressed as close as sardines in a tin, but more miserable, I suspected. The music stopped and the stout woman next to me left here seat.

She charged over to the fiddlers with her hand outstretched.

'At least we can breathe noo,' I said to Nancy; but her eyes were strained towards the lounge door like a prisoner under guard who spies an escape route.

'We'll go then,' I said, 'if that's whit ye want,' but I didn't move because at that moment who should I catch sight of but Dad, standing in the doorway holding a pint of beer.

'Wait a minute,' I said to Nancy, 'this is one o' the guys that knows Craig – the one with the business. He canny be far away.'

She muttered something under her breath, but I wasn't listening. I was on my feet and beckoning on my old friend. He came over and squeezed in beside me, his smile as bland as ever. He took a long pull at his pint, then put his tumbler on the table with a sigh of satisfaction and wiped his mouth. I wished I had one to go with it.

'This bloody place,' I said, 'takes you all day to get served.'

'So I've noticed,' he said distantly.

'Anyway,' I said, deciding not to beat about the bush, I saw the article in the paper about this Lifeline business. So I decided to take a dauner up here to see whit was doin'.' I added with a deprecating laugh, 'And maybe to get a job, if there wis one gaun, that is.'

'Is that so?' said Dad, looking quizzical.

'Oh, by the way,' I gestured towards Nancy, 'this is the girlfriend who's came alang wi' me. We've been campin' on the way here, as an excuse for a bit of a holiday.'

Dad leaned forward to say 'Howdy do,' which fell on deaf ears. Nancy had turned her head away.

'She's no' feelin' well,' I informed Dad, and thankfully called on the waiter who had entered. I ordered two pints of beer and asked Nancy what she wanted to drink. She said she was leaving. 'I can't stand any more of this place,' she announced, and gave Dad a tight smile on the way out.

'A very attractive girl, if ye don't mind me sayin' so,' said Dad.

'Aye,' I said, longing to run after her and tell her to be

reasonable and consider how lucky I was to meet Dad. But she had disappeared through the swinging door.

'At least you got the weather,' Dad was saying.

'How dae ye mean?'

'I mean for the campin'. You got good weather.'

Impatiently I said, 'It wisny bad, 'but the main thing is for you to tell me where Craig is, or Major Burns as he's named in the papers.'

Dad stared ahead, as if deaf. After the waiter had returned with the beer and I had paid him with the change in my pocket, which was just enough, I repeated my statement.

'Craig's gone,' Dad said.

'Gone? Whit dae ye mean, gone?'

'The last time I saw Craig wis ootside this pub when we were staunin' on the pavement discussing various matters. Then a car drew up and somebody called on him. I thought it wis tae ask him directions. Well, he got into the car. It drove away and I hivny seen him since.'

I stared hard into Dad's face. It struck me for the first time that without his bland smile his eyes appeared too close-set and his lips too thin for my liking.

I said, 'Ye must think I'm daft if ye expect me tae believe that.'

'I don't care whit ye believe,' he said, sounding insolent.

I drank some beer and informed him that if he didn't take me to Craig or whatever he was called, I might do something drastic, like kicking him very severely.

'Ye'll jist have tae dae that,' he replied, 'for I don't ken whaur he is.' In turn he drank his beer and banged his tumbler on the table in a righteous fashion. I thought maybe he was telling the truth.

'OK,' I said, 'but I still want tae know whit ye're a' up tae. You, McLerie and Craig, and in particular I want tae know how I wis bein' watched at the lodgin' hoose, and don't waste time in denyin' it.'

'All right,' said Dad, unperturbed. 'I'll no' deny that we had an interest in ye, up tae a point, but it never ran deep, ye ken. Ye jist happened tae arrive when we were lookin' for somebody tae stir things up.'

'How dae ye mean, stir things up?'

'Things like passin' roon pamphlets, speakin' on soap boxes, or daein' a bit o' hecklin' at political meetin's – stuff like that, ye ken?'

'I don't ken one bit,' I said.

Dad sighed. 'It's no' straightforward, right enough, but politics never are.'

'I think I know whit it's aboot,' I said. 'It's the National Front. Is that whit ye are?'

'No' really,' said Dad, looking more like his old affable self again. 'It's much mair important than the National Front.'

'Don't tell me it's the Secret Service?'

Dad hesitated, then said, 'I canny gie ye the whole story for I don't know it masel'. It stauns tae reason when ye're dealin' wi' somethin', say for example like the MI5, ye're only gaun tae know so much.'

'MI5?' I exclaimed.

'I'm no' sayin' it's MI5. I'm only gi'in' ye an example'

I stared hard at Dad for a few moments, wondering if he was taking the mickey out of me, especially when I remembered the rubber mask. 'Tell me,' I said, feeling tired and out of my depth and worried about Nancy, 'why dae ye want trouble stirred up in the first place?'

'The fact is,' said Dad, 'though ye micht no' believe me, but even in a great wee country like oor ain, folk are aye plottin' things. Ye micht say that there's always an undercurrent o' unrest against the wans at the tap.'

I nodded and said, 'It's no' surprisin' when ye consider how the wans at the bottom are treated.'

'Well, there ye are. There's always some that want tae dae somethin', but usually they don't bother until somebody comes alang and stirs it up. Afore ye know it there are organised groups tryin' to create disorder. Dae ye see whit I mean?'

'That's a bloody good idea,' I said. 'I'd support that. Is

that whit yous are – anarchists? Plantin' bombs and a' that?'

He chuckled. 'Oh naw, no' anarchists. We're no' in tae that kind o' thing. The opposite, fact.'

I said irritably, 'I wish ye'd come right oot and tell me exactly whit ye are in tae. I've come a long way tae see Colin Craig, or should I say Major Burns. He promised me a job and that's a ' I'm interested in, so whit the hell is this Lifeline aboot anyway?'

He shook his head and sighed. 'Patience is no' a virtue o' the young, I ken, but if ye're that keen tae know I'll tell ye this much, for mind I only know so much masel'. Lifeline is the code-name for wan o' the latest drives in stirrin' things up, and that's whit me and Craig are paid tae dae – forbye gettin' recruits tae help us, and that's where you'd have come in. It's a method whereby we can get a' the troublemakers to expose themselves right away. Ye see, we'd be infiltratin' wi' them and we'd know in advance whit their plans wir. At least, that wis the idea, but the plan has been scrapped for this area meanwhile, since the folk here are no' sae easily roused. Likely Craig's been sent doon south where there's mair unrest.'

It struck me Dad could be telling the truth, otherwise why should he make up such an unlikely story? But true or not, this encounter was a blow to any prospects of a job, and outside all this I was worrying about Nancy. She had been in a grim mood when she left.

'Well, it's a' one tae me whether it's been scrapped or no',' I said, 'I widny work for you or Craig if that's whit yer game is.'

'Whit game?' he asked slyly.

'Whit ye were explainin'. Gettin' folked stirred up, as you describe it. Onyway, I'm no' sure I get the point of it.'

'Well,' said Dad patiently, like a teacher dealing with a thick pupil, 'we tip the leaders aff tae the polis and they get done for sedition, which carries a heavy sentence. It's troubled times nooadays, and it'll get worse. There are them that want tae bring doon the government, and oor job's tae spot the dangerous wans afore they can start their ploys.'

'So,' I said, 'we set traps for oor ain folk.'

'We set traps for them that are a potential danger tae the country. We're daein' decent folk a favour,' said Dad indignantly.

Depression swept over me as I sat with my head in my hands trying to sort things out. No matter how I looked at it there was nothing in Dad's account of Lifeline that I liked, nor was there anything now about Dad that I liked, or his accomplices and their peculiar business. From what he was saying I guessed they were nothing better than informers creating circumstances they could inform on. I felt like bashing him. I had decided to leave before I did so when Dad said, 'Ye're lookin' kind o' seedy. Wid ye like somethin' a wee tate stronger than beer?'

It occurred to me that I might as well get some Dutch courage in order to face Nancy, who might not be easy to talk round. 'If ye like,' I said. 'As usual I'm skint.'

He ordered whisky for both of us, then said after we had been served, 'It's a damned shame that a fine big fella like yersel' has to be shoved on the scrap-heap.'

I nodded absently and asked him what had happened to McLerie. Had he gone with Craig?

Dad chuckled and said, 'McLerie's in jile. He was a leader o' an organised group that played intae oor haunds. He wis an activist afore we met him.'

'I thought he wis Craig's man,' I said, surprised.

'So did he. He thought the sun shone oot Craig's arse. It wis laughable to see how much he trusted him, but he wis one o' these immigrants frae across the water. His pub wis a shelter for the assassins that are bred there. He actually thought Lifeline wis tae be a base for a' kinds o' terrorists, and he selt his pub tae come this length. But ye'll no' see him for a while, if ever.'

I smiled weakly at Dad and swallowed my whisky in one go, hoping it would settle the churning in my stomach. I told him all I had wanted was a straightforward job as a brickie. I doubted that I had the temperament for anything else. Dad watched me intently as I spoke. His eyes and lips were curiously moist.

'Ye're much too modest,' he said. 'I think ye'd be useful at a lot o' things. If ye stick wi' me for a wee while I'll be able to put ye on tae somethin' good wi' plenty money in it.' He then squeezed my hand, which I had innocently placed near his on top of the table. I swiped it off so violently that I hurt my knuckles. Dad flinched and groaned.

Roughly I asked him if he wasn't worried that I would repeat all he had told me to folk of consequence, who would possibly create a big stink about it.

He said, still looking pained, 'But who'd believe a hobo like yersel', and where's the proof, if ye could even catch us?'

I thought this over and decided that he was right. I even began to wonder if his tale was true. Dad was a very devious man, and maybe even a cracked-up shot; but whatever the truth of it was, it was certain to be as unpleasant as the touch of his hand. As for Craig, if he could stomach a guy like Dad, he was capable of anything. They were all bad medicine, including McLerie, even if he was in jail. The important thing now was to find Nancy.

'Excuse me,' I said to Dad, 'I'll have tae leave afore I puke all over ye. But let me warn ye, if I meet ye ootside I might be tempted tae stamp ye intae the ground like the black beetle ye resemble.'

His composure had returned. When I left he was smiling blandly towards the fiddlers, who had now begun to play again.

Later in the evening Nancy and I were standing inside a shop door not far from a bus stop. After I had left the pub it hadn't taken me long to find her. Lornack wasn't such a big place. She had been staring in at a shop window full of souvenirs.

'Buyin' something?' I had asked.

She shook her head and told me she didn't want anything to remind her of this place, or for that matter any part of the expedition. Besides, there wasn't much money left and she was going home.

'But ye canny.'

'But I can.' She gave me a look of pity, or maybe it was contempt, but I knew she wasn't joking.

'I'll be stayin',' I said, 'for there's nothin' to go back for.'

'I thought you might,' she said, and walked away.

I had followed her round the town giving her reasons why she shouldn't go. In my heart I knew they weren't good ones. Even as I spoke I was gasping for a couple of jugfuls to get the adrenalin started, which had expired from the time I left Dad. Now I was asking her how she knew a bus would be leaving this one-eyed hole for anywhere.

'I enquired when you were in the pub.'

'Dae ye have to go?'

'Yes,' she said.

With her mouth set firm and her chin held high I had never seen her look so good. Perhaps it was the effect of the neon light from the shop window, but recently it had seemed to me she had looked better with every day that passed, and this was to be the last one.

Desperately I said, 'There'll be nae mair pubs from now on, if ye stay.'

She frowned and shook her head. In the dusk her eyes seemed smudged.

'It's no use. I'm going home.'

'I thought ye loved me.'

She must have thought hard about this because she took her time answering. Finally she said that perhaps she did, but she wasn't sure. She couldn't judge matters clearly at the moment. Then she burst out passionately, 'It's the way you act. You've no consideration. I can't stand it. I was brought up to believe that consideration is very important, and I think that's true.'

The expression 'brought up' defeated me. It conjured up the opposite situation of being 'dragged up' which I must have presented to her in the course of our relationship. I made another try. 'I promise I'm finished wi' the booze. Cross ma heart.' I made the sign.

'You're not even a Catholic,' she said.

'Ye don't have tae be,' I began to say when I heard the noise of the bus in the distance. 'Stay one mair day,' I pleaded. 'Everythin' will look different in the mornin', especially when the sun's shinin'. I can tell by the sky it's gaun tae be good.'

She fumbled in her purse and gave me a fiver, saying, 'Don't drink it all. You'll need it for fares.'

She picked up her rucksack and swung it on to her shoulder before I could help her. The headlights from the bus were upon us, blinding us. She stepped onto the platform and turned round to stare at me so miserably you would have thought I was forcing her to go. I waited at the halt until the bus was a speck in the distance, then I moved off. As I headed for the first pub – not the Locheil Bar, though, since I had no wish to see Dad again – I thought I could still smell the fresh cut grass perfume of her hair.

I cut through a cobbled lane for no other reason than to give me time to compose the expression on my face, which I suspected was one of severe pain. By the time I reached the end of the lane which led into a main street my face had stiffened.

I had spied two figures crossing the street beyond the lane. Even in the dark I knew it was Dad and Colin Craig. Partners in dubious dealings as they were, in every outward aspect they looked ill-matched. I headed for the street to confirm what I already knew and saw the short squat figure of Dad scuttling along the pavement hastily to keep up with the longer and steadier footsteps of Craig.

For a moment I hesitated. One part of my brain said forget them. In every way they were bad medicine. Another more urgent part of my brain wanted explanations and compensation, particularly from Craig. For the short time I had known him I had liked him, and admired his cool and upper-class style – so much that I had followed him on this wild goose chase, dragging Nancy with me, on the strength of a vague promise of work. And for my pains I had lost Nancy. What made it worse was that I had always professed to despise rich and successful types like Craig. Not that Craig struck me now as being rich and successful. If what Dad said was true he was no more than a villain – but worse than the average, being an agitator and informer. Whatever he was, the fact remained that I had been duped. I decided it was imperative to let them know that I wasn't quite the country boy they took me for.

I caught Craig by the shoulder as they turned round a corner where the pavement and the street began to slope downwards.

'Remember me?' I asked.

He studied me for a moment with one eyebrow raised but otherwise unsurprised. 'Certainly,' he said, adding pleasantly, 'How strange to find you in this Godforsaken place. You are on holiday, perhaps?'

'No' really,' I said.

'He's been trailin' efter us,' said Dad, giving me a mean look.

'Trailing after us,' said Craig, sounding amused.

Patiently I said, 'If ye remember, ye once promised me a job, and so naturally when I saw yer photo in the paper under the name of Major Burns askin' for folk tae join this Lifeline project, I decided to take the plunge and come up. So whit aboot it?'

Dad addressed Craig. 'See him. He's lookin' for trouble. I've telt him there's nae job.'

'Is that right, Craig?' I asked. 'There's nae job?'

Craig shrugged. 'Sorry, young man. Just one of those deals that didn't work out. Pity your journey was for nothing, and such a long way too.'

'It wis an experience,' I said airily. 'One that I'll keep in mind, especially efter whit Dad telt me.'

'And what did Dad tell you,' said Craig, with a swift glance at Dad.

'Spyin' on folk is whit ye're intae, and then informin' on them.'

'I never telt him that,'said Dad indignantly. 'He's makin' it up.'

'He telt me, as well, that McLerie's in jail and it wis you two that put him there. He telt me a lot of other things that were hard tae believe. I would be obliged if you could put me in the picture a wee bit better.'

There was a pause during which Craig regarded Dad steadily, then regarded me steadily. I noticed a pub across the street with fancy stained-glass windows. Somebody entered the swing doors and I heard a hum of male voices. It looked cheerful. I decided to head for it soon with my fiver.

Craig said in a colder voice than formerly. 'Lifeline was a perfectly legitimate venture which did not come to pass. If Dad told you otherwise, it is untrue; but then he always had a vivid imagination, because of his theatrical connections, no doubt. Some people might call him a liar.' Then he addressed Dad, 'Isn't that right?'

'It is,' said Dad.

'That's too bad,' I said, 'because it so happens I believed every word that Dad telt me; and it also so happens trailin' yous wisny ma only reason for comin' up here. I've got relatives in this toon who are a very close lot, very sectarian they are, in fact real troublemakers. They would knife you as quick as look at you, and see that pub ower there, that's where they drink.'

When Craig automatically looked towards the pub I was pointing at, I caught him with a hard blow to the side of the face. He stumbled sideways and I caught him with another blow. I wasn't worrying what Dad would do. From the side of my eye I saw him scuttling down the sloping pavement. Give Craig his due, he attempted to come back at me, but he had lost the place. A few more blows and he was on the pavement saying, 'No more.' I must admit I administered another couple of kicks, which wasn't sporting, and probably done for the loss of Nancy, which if you look at it truthfully wasn't entirely his fault. Before I left him on the pavement, still conscious, I put my hand inside his well-tailored jacket and took out a wallet containing a cheque book, which was of no use to me, but the twenty-pound note inside it was. I returned the wallet to his jacket pocket while he was feebly attempting to rise. It was the same wallet he had had at the peace festival, the one with the initials A.R.B.

'For auld times' sake,' I said, and headed for the cheerful pub across the street.

CHAPTER 13

I stayed in the pub long enough to drink two whiskies. I was aware of curious stares in my direction, perhaps because I exuded an air of violence, or perhaps because it was obvious from my rucksack that I was a camper – sometimes not a popular thing to be. I couldn't have stopped long in any case, being haunted by the thought of Nancy arriving back in Lornack in order to give me one more chance. This didn't prevent me from ordering a bottle of whisky as a bulwark against the pain of disappointment on that score.

The barman avoided my eye as he served me, staring at my bruised knuckles instead.

'Jist had an accident,' I explained, and left quickly before he could say anything.

I wandered the shaded streets, stopping every so often to drink from the bottle, thinking it had been absurd to consider she would return, but caring less about it the more I drank. A policeman approached me and asked where I was going, at the same time frowning at the bottle.

'Lookin' for ma mate,' I replied. 'We're daein' a bit of hikin' and I've lost him somewhere on the road.'

Now, looking at my rucksack, he said. 'You'd better be warned that there is no camping allowed either here or within the vicinity, so get as far away as you can or I'll be taking you in.'

'In whit direction?'

He pointed up the road, saying, 'Just go.'

I walked a few yards then shouted back to him, 'I didny like this place onyway.'

Within half an hour I had left the suburbs and saw ahead, in the moonlight, a stretch of fields on each side of the road. I squeezed through a gap in the hedge, unpacked my rucksack and discovered I was in possession of two sleeping bags, a frying pan, but minus a tent. The tent would be far away in the bus inside Nancy's rucksack. I decided that it was no great loss. The less I carried, the better. In the morning I would dump the frying pan and the stove. I wouldn't be frying anything anyway. So I settled down inside the sleeping bag, and with the other one rolled up as a bolster for my back, I fell asleep, still holding the bottle.

I was woken by the noise of a passing lorry on the other side of the hedge. I saw the sky was dull, but I thought the weather would be good enough for walking. I stood up to shiver in the cool air, pleasantly surprised to see that there was still whisky left in the bottle. Things weren't so bad after all. I packed my rucksack, leaving out the stove and the frying pan (though not, after all, without some regret) and set off along the road on the other side of the hedge, carrying the bottle in one hand. I had reached the temperance hotel where Nancy and I had been dumped by the woman in the car when I remembered I should have bought fags and some instant food like bread and cheese before leaving civilisation; but no way was I going to go back. I might be tempted to take the bus. The idea of arriving in the big city without Nancy was unbearable. I felt I had to walk back over this lonely space until I came to terms with my unhappiness – like Moses in the desert, who had been another screwed up guy, I thought, smiling to myself at the unlikely comparison.

I walked on, endlessly it seemed, wishing I knew how far I had travelled. Two cars passed me on the road. One of them slowed down as if to give me a lift. I sat by the side of the road, yards back, to show that I wasn't interested. I regretted this immediately the car moved off. I could have asked how far I had come from Lornack. Yet, what did it matter? I wasn't heading for any place in particular. It was just hard to keep this in mind, I thought, as I took a swig from the bottle.

It took some effort to stand up and move again. I began to sing as I walked, composing my own tunes and rhymes and sipping from the bottle at intervals. By the time I reached the stony valley I was staggering from exhaustion and booze. I sat between the rocks, hunched up, clasping my knees, watching big black birds circling high above my head. Buzzards, I thought gloomily, and fell asleep.

This rest gave me the strength to reach the cliffs overlooking the sea. I put the whisky bottle to my lips, but found it was empty. Enraged, I threw it over the cliff edge. It smashed upon the rocks and the seagulls rose up screaming.

'I'm sorry,' I called to them, and sank to my knees. I felt tears stinging my eyes, which proved that I was at a very low ebb indeed. I decided to rest on this spot for the night, whenever that might be; but anyway, night or day, I could go no further. Though I was slightly deranged at that moment, I had the sense to put one sleeping bag inside the other to make sure of a warm bed. After crawling inside I fell asleep, lulled by the lapping sound of the waves on the rocks, and dreamt of Nancy.

The sky was clear when I forced myself out of my thick sleep to face the strong wind blowing over the headland. Down below the waves roared.

I turned away from the bleak scene and dragged my gear well back from the cliff edge in case a gust of wind blew it over. I wrapped it up, but it was a laborious business for I was weak with hunger as well as stiff with cold, and to make it worse my fags were crushed and sodden. I began to think I might die in this wilderness and no one would know. Anyway, no one would miss me, apart from my mother, and even that was doubtful. If Nancy thought of me at all, it would likely be as an association worse than the one she had with the Canadian guy. Strangely enough, it was at this desperate stage that an idea entered my head, in the way a drowning man in the sea below might clutch at a piece of driftwood. It was this: if I could manage it, I would head for the Auchenachen Inn, with its lounge of pale plastic divans and tumblers on the ceiling, where the buxom hostess Jessie might serve me with a plate of soup, or even two plates of soup. Despite her slap on my cheek before I was flung out of the inn, I was struck now with a clear impression that she had liked me up until that stage. Besides, I had money to pay for a meal, which might make a difference, and I was alone, another point in my favour. I laughed aloud and said, looking up at the sky, still being weak in the head as well as the body, 'Thanks for the sign.'

If I hadn't had the gumption to buy a loaf and a pint of milk from a suspicious-faced farmer's wife, I believe the buzzards would have got me in the end. As it was, I reached the reception desk at the Auchenachen Inn in a poor condition. I could hardly stand. I rang the bell three times before Jessie came through and said, looking over my head, 'Sorry, we're not open till six.'

I clutched the desk with both hands, saying, 'Can I sit doon somewhere. I think I'm gaun tae faint.'

Immediately she pulled me into the lounge, where I collapsed on one of the pale plastic divans. From a distance I heard her say, 'Are you the fellow who was camping with his girlfriend?' Then I passed out. I was returned to consciousness by the sound of Jessie placing cutlery on the table in front of me.

I sat up awkwardly and said, 'Sorry aboot the commotion. I'm thinkin' it wis because I hudny ate for a long time.'

'I'm thinking that too,' she said, without looking at me, and straightening a knife with deliberation. Then she marched off, swinging her hips in a businesslike manner.

Doubting that the cutlery was for me, I drank some water from a glass on the table. I thought this was all I would get, but she came back carrying a plate of steaming food.

'Eat this slowly,' she said, 'for I'm thinking that your belly will have shrunk and it would be bad for you to gobble.'

She watched me as I ate, tutting if I began to gobble. It was hard not to, the food was so fantastic. When I had finished, I asked her how much I owed.

'Pay me later,' she said with a smile. Then she became serious and asked why I had come to be in such a state, and why I was alone. I gave her a brief version of the affair, leaving out Craig and Dad, and saying more or less that my girlfriend had left me because I drunk too much booze. She shrugged and said that from what she remembered of my girlfriend, she had looked the type that would be hard to please on any score.

'Perhaps,' I said distantly, not wanting to pursue the subject.

'I'll tell you what,' she said later, when I had almost fallen asleep over the table as she spoke, 'go up to the room facing you on the first landing and have a lie down. You can't be sleeping here when the customers arrive.'

She led me by the hand out of the lounge and up the stairs, then shoved me in the direction of the room. I wanted to kiss her hand with gratitude, but she had vanished back down the stairs. Inside, the curtains were drawn, making the place dim, but I could see the shape of a bed. I stumbled towards it gladly, remembering, just in time, to take off all my clothes, except my underpants, in case I dirtied the sheets.

I woke suddenly. Something or someone had disturbed me. It seemed dark, as if it was late in the evening, though with the curtains drawn the room had been dark enough when I had stumbled into bed earlier. Then there was a sound, like a suppressed giggle.

'Who is it?' I asked.

'It's only Jessie,' came the reply.

A light was switched on. Now I saw the place clearly. I stared at a light oak wall unit, a writing bureau, a washbasin and the green velvet curtains that were closed – all very elegant, but it was Jessie who riveted my attention, standing next to a lampshade on the table beside the bed. She wore a black filmy garment which barely covered her chest. She leaned over me, her hair touching my cheek, and said, 'Are you feeling all right, dear?'

'Fine,' I said. 'I wis aboot tae get up,' and rose some inches off the bed to convey this.

'Now,' she said, pushing me down again, 'don't get excited. I've only came to give you something that will make you feel a lot better. In fact it will make us both feel a lot better. I've been a bit down in the dumps myself lately.'

As she headed for the writing bureau I saw the outline of her figure through the filmy garment, which made me agitated, though I wasn't sure exactly in what way. She opened a door in the bureau and brought out a fancy-shaped bottle, along with two glasses and a tray.

'It's some wine I've been saving for a special occasion, and I'm thinking this is as good an occasion as any.'

She put the tray and glasses on the table and began to pour. I saw it was a white wine and suspected it wasn't going to be strong enough for the occasion, as far as I was concerned. I drank it quickly and said, 'Very nice,' wondering how I could escape from the room without showing my nearly naked body as well as appearing ungrateful for her extreme hospitality.

'My, my,' she said. 'You are a quick drinker. No wonder your girlfriend took the hump.'

'Sorry,' I said, unable to look her in the eye, 'I wis chokin' wi' thirst.'

'Don't apologise,' she said with a throaty chuckle, 'I'm not short of a few bottles. But next time drink it slow.'

I was about to explain that I wasn't partial to white wine, when she said, 'Do you mind if I sit on the bed? It's not easy to drink standing up.'

Quickly I moved nearer to the wall, wondering what I had let myself in for. She sat with her back facing me. Her skin was very white and I noticed that there was a mole on her left shoulder, which I couldn't help admiring. There were a lot of things about her that I couldn't help admiring, but not so close at hand. Then she gave a big sigh, as if she knew what I was thinking, which moved me to ask if she was feeling OK.

'As a matter of fact,' she said, looking round at me, 'this is not comfortable either. I'll have to bring my legs in, otherwise I'll get a crick in my neck if I speak to you.'

Before I could answer she had swung her legs onto the bed, stretching them out so that we were lying side by side with only the blankets between us.

'That's better,' she said, and splashed more wine in the glasses. I drank mine, forgetting to be slow. Again I tried to think of some way of escaping, but I was becoming dazed. The wine was stronger than I had judged.

Then she said quietly, 'Perhaps you want me to go?'

This question confused me, for at that particular moment I hadn't been thinking of anything at all.

'No' really,' I said.

'What is it then? You're not saying much.'

I couldn't think of anything to say, being distracted by the sight of her plump but shapely legs and the red varnish on her toenails.

'Maybe it's because – ' I began, unable to think clearly

what it was because of.

'Because of what?' she said. 'Tell me. You're not afraid of me, surely?'

As she regarded me with concern I certainly couldn't think of any reason to be afraid of her, I could only say, 'Maybe it's because you're lyin' here with hardly anythin' on. Whit am I supposed to think?'

Her concern faded. 'You can think what you like, but I bet if your girlfriend was here you'd know what to think.'

'She wis different.'

'Different! I'm sure she was, leaving you the way she did.'

'I telt ye afore, it wis ma fault.'

'H'mm,' said Jessie, sounding bored.

After a strained pause I said, 'It doesny mean to say that because she wis different she was any better than you.'

At that Jessie moved closer to me so that her bare shoulder touched mine.

'I see that you've finished your drink again. What a terrible man you are.'

This time I drank only half of the wine she poured. It was getting more potent by the minute. Jessie put her glass on the table.

'Do you mind if I get under the blankets?' she asked. 'I'm fair freezing.'

By this time I had no qualms about anything. 'Get under,' I said and was immediately excited by the feel of her hips on mine when she moved in.

'I was beginning to think,' she said, snuggling close to me, 'that you only came here to be fed.'

I leaned over and put my glass on the table, saying, 'There was that, I admit, but I thought ye might have slapped me again if I tried for anything else.'

'Oh that,' she said. 'It was only to impress McFarlane who would have been in a terrible mood all night if I hadn't.'

I put my arms round Jessie's shoulder, not caring about McFarlane, and considering I could do a lot worse than to stay on here and settle down with Jessie until such times as the building trade took a turn for the better.

'What you need,' said Jessie turning towards me and wrapping her arms round my neck, 'is a great big cuddle.'

After that we came together easily. In fact we came together twice. I didn't quite make it the second time. It was spoiled by a fleeting memory of Nancy in my arms. Jessie didn't seem to notice.

'There's jist one mair thing I'd like,' I said later as we were finishing the last of the wine.

'Not again, surely?'

'I huvny had a fag for days and I'm fair gaspin'.'

'There's always something you're wanting,' said Jessie.

She rose from the bed, opened the door in the writing bureau and threw me over a packet of twenty Benson & Hedges along with a box of matches.

'That's a queer writin' bureau,' I said jokingly, surprised that she was making no move to come back in beside me. Not that I was bothering too much. At the moment I didn't fancy another session. But I didn't like the way she was looking at me very contemplatively.

'Whit's wrang?' I asked.

'Nothing really, but I'll have to get downstairs. It must be well past opening time and the customers will be furious.'

I thought she was starting to look a bit furious herself. I said evenly, 'Well, if ye must go, there's nae way oot o' it.'

I took a puff of the fag. It almost took the breath from me, I had been so long without one.

I said, as she continued to stare at me through eyelashes that had become gritty with mascara, 'but I'll come doon later if ye like and gie ye a haun'.'

'You can't stay here. I've to get the room ready for the next visitor.'

For a moment I thought she was joking; then I knew she wasn't when she added accusingly, 'And these sheets will need changing.'

'You mean, I've to go right now.'

'I'll give you ten minutes. Meantime I'm off to get dressed.'

'Wait a minute,' I called, as she turned to leave, 'is that a' ye've got to say?'

'And what am I supposed to say?' she asked with astonishment.

I knew there was no chance of it now, but I said anyway, 'I hoped you might gie me a job – barman, bouncer, or maybe collectin' tumblers, anything like that.'

'A job!' she said. 'And how could I give you a job, with the place not paying as it is, and it soon to be closed for the winter.'

Then she took a few paces nearer the bed and said in a more conciliatory way, 'Look, even if I could give you a job, I know you wouldn't stop long. I can tell you're not the hotel type and I do my own bouncing.'

'I could learn,' I said, encouraged by her softening attitude.

'You're much too rugged looking, if you know what I mean. Hotel staff, particularly the men, are required to be smooth.' She laughed, looking more like the Jessie I had lain with. 'Maybe that's why I wanted a shot of you in bed. It's not often I come across a rugged fellow like yourself.'

'Is that all it was – a shot?'

'Listen,' she said. 'I've got my business to attend to. I can't give it up for any young fellow who happens to come along. I've given you too much of my time already.' She sighed, 'But that's hotel life for you, never a minute to spare for pleasure.'

I nodded my head in sympathy, and told her I would leave immediately.

'Finish your cigarette first, and take my advice. Go back home and get on with your life. You look as though you'll be a big success one day. Make it up with your girlfriend, if you can. Likely it was only a lovers' tiff you had.'

As she left she said, 'Good luck, and keep the packet.'

After she'd gone I jumped from the bed, put on my clothes and gave myself a wash in the spotless washbasin. I left nearly all the money I possessed on the table, knowing Jessie would be back to tidy the room. When all was said and done, she deserved it. And anyway, the place wasn't paying. She would need it. She was right about me not being the hotel type.

Ten minutes later I was walking the pitch-black trail, hoping to find some hedge or bush where I could bed down for the night, and thinking that the best thing I could do was to become a tramp.

CHAPTER 14

I was back home sitting in my mother's plastic easy chair, feeling like an intruder. Opposite me my mother sat frowning.

She said, 'I didny expect ye back sae soon. Whit's happened?'

I thought her appearance was as drab as ever, with her straight hair, crossover apron and slippers burst at the toes. Yet I've seen her look fairly spruce when she's been forced out to events such as weddings and funerals, with her hair frizzed and wearing the fur coat she got from the Oxfam shop, looking very impressive, and young for her forty-odd years.

‘Are ye no’ pleased tae see me?’ I asked.

‘Of course, but there’s nothin’ much tae eat, apart frae sausages, and I suppose ye’ll be hungry.’

‘Sausages will be fine.’

I had actually had nothing to eat for twenty-four hours, except for bread and cheese from a lorry driver. He had picked me up a few miles outside Grinstone and dropped me near my home town. At the time I had considered this a piece of luck. Now I wasn’t so sure. If I had hiked it all the way I might have come to a sticky end, which would have been all for the best the way things were going. Or I might have, through necessity, been forced to become a poacher or a sheep rustler, like some guys have done, and finished up wealthy.

My mother disappeared into the kitchen. I looked around furtively. The room was shabbier than I had remembered. There was a fusty smell that I hadn’t noticed before. Perhaps it had always been there. When she returned with a cup of tea and thick sausage sandwiches on a plate I said, ‘It’s time ye were gettin’ a shift oot this place. It’s rotten wi’ damp.’

‘So, it’s no’ good enough for ye,’ she said as she thrust the cup into my hand, spilling tea on my denims.

‘I couldny imagine bringin’ onyone in here, even for a sing-song.’

‘So,’ she said, with her hand on her hips, ‘ye’ve got haud o’ some fancy wumman.’

‘Don’t be daft. I’m no’ blamin’ you,’ I said, thinking I had gone too far. ‘Ye dae yer best.’

‘I should think so,’ she said, then declared I was likely right about the state of the place. It badly needed decorating. She would buy paper and paint from the co-operative and I could get started first thing in the morning. That is, she added tentatively, if I had any money to spare.

‘Hardly a bean,’ I told her. ‘The entire venture wis a washoot.’

‘That’s a pity,’ she said, leaning back in her chair and looking worried.

'At least it wis an experience,' I said, with some defiance.

I sat back and swung a leg over the chair as she stared pensively into the unlit grate of the fireplace, her face sad but resigned.

'Cheer up,' I said. 'It might never happen.'

'The thing is,' she began, 'I don't know how I'm gaun tae manage noo that you're hame.'

'Don't worry. I'll get somethin' even if it's only broo money. Ye see, I had a job for a wee while up north, and I didny pack it in. I got paid aff. That makes a difference.'

'Does it?' she said quietly, and regarded me with the commiseration one gives an invalid.

'Whit's wrang?'

She sighed. 'I've often thought I should have had ye adopted when ye were a wean.'

'Adopted?'

'If ye'd been adopted by posh folk ye could have been a doctor or a civil servant by this time.'

'Whit's brought this on?' I asked angrily.

'There's nae chance for fellas like you nooadays. Ye need friends in high places.'

'Look,' I said sternly. 'I wid hate tae be a doctor or a civil servant. I'd rather be who I am, even if I am on the dole.'

'Is that right?' said my mother, smiling and flushed as if relieved. 'I've often thought aboot that – '

I interrupted her, 'Jist you get intae the kitchen and find me anither piece wi' something on it.'

The next morning I was dragging my footsteps on the road to the Labour Exchange when I accidentally came to the Paxton Arms, a pub I used to frequent. Its outer shade of faded pink was the same, perhaps flaking more than before, but the worst aspect about it was that it was closed. I asked a guy wandering past with a black dog on a leash if it was shut for good. He said, with a touch of hostility, 'It's only because there's nae giros delivered on a Monday. It'll be open the morra.'

I walked off in the opposite direction to conceal the fact I was heading for the broo because sometimes I have my pride. I arrived at the derelict drive where the squatters hang out, hiding behind smashed windows with the torn curtains blowing through the gaps like streamers.

Half-way along the drive I saw a gap in the building heaped with char, as if connections had been deliberately severed by fire. Then I came to a doorway where a guy was hunkered down spreading out fag-ends on the step. It was big Mick, an acquaintance of mine who was very partial to the wine of South Africa. I remembered that I owed him a fiver from way back. It was doubtful if he would remember this. A lot of booze would have been drunk since then. I had no real notion for his company, but I was stirred by the thought that he might have a bottle of plonk in the pocket of his long black coat, which he wore in all seasons. I called his name. He stared up at me vacantly. Then he began to laugh in a wheezing manner, like Motley the cartoon dog. When he shook my hands his fingers felt like something retrieved from the earth, cold and clammy. There was no bulge in his pocket that I could see, so I told him that I was in a hurry; but he continued to grip my hand with surprising strength.

'Christ man, I thought you were aff tae Australia,' he said, pumping my arm and wheezing sorely. I asked him bluntly if either he or his mate Baldy, another acquaintance of mine, had any booze to spare, since I didn't feel so good. He rubbed his chin with an air of surprise. 'Baldy?' he said. 'He's been deid for a while. Did ye no' hear he wis burnt.'

'Burnt!' I repeated, having a fleeting image of a martyr at the stake.

'He lit a fire in the buildin' tae make some tea, and the place went up like a tinder-box. Luckily I wis away for a cerry oot at the time.'

Mick then took a fit of coughing, and asked me if I had a fag to spare to settle his throat.

'I haveny even got a match,' I explained.

He shrugged and turned back to his heap of fag-ends. I knelt down beside him. He picked out two of the freshest and handed me one, then asked if I would like to come in for a drink.

'In where?' I asked, squinting upwards.

He kicked open a door behind. I followed him over piles of rubble into a room strewn with more rubble. A blanket was spread out in front of a fireplace heaped with ash. A strong smell of urine assailed my nostrils.

'No' very fancy,' said Mick, 'but it's cheery enough when I get the fire gaun.'

'I'd rather ye didny light a fire,' I said, thinking of Baldy.

He brought a bottle out from under the blanket and told me to have a gargle. It was a strange colour, a mixture of brown and green. I asked him if it was a home brew. He said that he wasn't sure as he had found it up the park. I said at that rate I wouldn't bother. He put the bottle to his mouth for a while, then told me it was the best stuff he had tasted for a long time. 'Go on, man,' he said, 'it'll no' kill ye.'

I wasn't sure about that but he was right about the booze. It was so strong that it brought the tears to my eyes. 'It's a liqueur, wan o' them fancy drinks that they serve in wee thin glasses big enough for a dwarf,' I explained.

After another couple of swallows each Mick became drunk. He began to sway and mumble.

'Are ye OK?' I asked.

'Sure I'm OK.' He fixed me with his bloodshot eyes. 'I've jist minded that you owe me a fiver. Ye borrowed it afore ye left for Australia.'

'You mean up north.'

'I don't care where it wis. Ye owe me a fiver,' said Mick, his voice thick but explicit.

'I thought it wis Baldy I owed the fiver.'

He thought over this remark and said, 'Maybe it wis so ye can gie me the money and I'll pass it on.'

'I thought ye said Baldy wis deid.'

'Who telt ye that?' he said, and took another swallow without offering me any.

'Is he deid or is he no'?' I asked impatiently. He was hold ing the bottle about an inch away from his eyes in order to gauge what amount of the liqueur remained. 'Maybe he's deid, but I'm no',' he said.

'Cheerio, Mick.' I turned away to find the exit. 'I've got better things tae dae than listen tae your ravings.'

He shouted, 'Fuck aff and leave me alane. Ye don't want me, but ye want ma drink.'

I thought, as I climbed over the heaps of plaster on the way out, that if I had any conscience at all I should report Mick to the social workers, or any kind of authority that took care of down and outs. But who was I to play God when I could scarcely take care of myself. Besides, he wouldn't thank me for it.

I didn't go near the Labour Exchange after that. The encounter with Mick had depressed me. When I returned to the house my mother asked me if I had been drinking. She was sure she could smell it off my breath. 'It's pineapple juice,' I said, 'it smells like drink.'

'Is that so?' she said, surprised.

I told her that there had been a long queue at the broo, but I would definitely go early the next morning.

'Jist as well ye didny wait,' she said. 'Duds Smith wants tae see ye. He might have a job for ye.'

'Duds the ragman. I canny see me shoutin' any auld rags through a tin trumpet.'

'Duds is in big business noo. He moved oot his council hoose intae a semi-detached. His wife walks aboot in a purple trooser outfit wi' her hair dyed blonde. It disny suit her.'

'Good luck to him, but I'm a brickie no' a hawker.' I turned up the television in order to finish the subject.

My mother turned it down again and said, 'Ye're no' likely tae be a brickie the way things are gaun nooadays, so ye'd better think again on Duds's offer. It's only because I'm pally wi' his wife that he's gi'en you the chance.'

'Did ye go crawlin' tae Duds on ma behalf?'

'I widny call it crawlin'. I'd call it havin' influence. It appears I'm the only one you know that has it.'

Duds Smith's scrapyard had stretched to double its original

size. The old conglomeration of rags, copper, cookers and lawnmowers had been replaced by four big caravans, all painted yellow and with flowered curtains to match.

'Whit dae ye think o' them?' said Duds, brandishing a brush dripping with yellow paint. His style hadn't altered any. He wore the same dusty velour hat and baggy strides shoved into wellingtons. He was a wee fat man, with a nose and complexion typical of a son of the Levant race, though he maintained his origins were Irish.

'They're fabulous,' I said. 'They must cost a bomb.'

'Only three hunner quid. They're auld caravans tarted up a bit. I've selt two already.'

'Three hunner,' I said. 'Who's got that kind o' money aboot here?'

'Them that's got their redundancy money. Whit could be a better buy than a holiday hoose on the coast for only three hunner?'

'Right enough,' I said.

'And the beauty o' it is, if they canny keep up the site dues next year, havin' blown their cash by that time, I can buy the same caravan back for next tae nothin'.'

I was doubtful of his ethics, but I had to acknowledge his business sense.

I said, 'Ye could sell sand in the Sahara,' adding, 'I widny mind a caravan masel', though.'

'So,' said Duds after a pause, 'can ye drive? I need a man to deliver the caravans doon tae the coast on a low-loadin' truck.'

'Sure I can drive.' Actually I had driven an old banger once and had been stopped by the law. I considered the experience adequate enough. 'I haveny got a drivin' licence.'

'Nae problem. I can always buy wan,' said Duds.

He mentioned the amount of money I would earn. It was a lot less than what I had received on the building site. I told him this and he threw in the offer of a caravan reduced by fifty pounds, which I could pay for in instalments. I hesitated because I considered that it was a come-down to work for

Duds and I didn't really fancy driving a low-loader down to the coast.

'Let me know by the efternoon,' said Duds, 'otherwise I'll have tae send for ma brither-in-law.'

I entered the Labour Exchange and walked past the queue waiting on the bench as though I had an appointment. I banged on the counter. The clerk came through from the back premises yawning, and then asked me if I had waited my turn. 'Sure,' I said. 'I'm fed up waitin'. I thought ye were away for a kip.'

He frowned and asked me what I wanted.

'A job,' I said. 'Preferably as a brickie.'

He sighed and took out a form from a drawer. 'If you want to sign on, fill up this form.'

I asked him for a pen. He told me to sign it at home.

'How can I no' sign it here and save the footwear.'

'It's the rules,' he said wearily.

'I'll gie ye back yer pen, honest.'

He continued to shake his head as though he had some kind of palsy. Someone on the bench called, 'That guy's dodged his turn.'

'If that's true go and sit on the bench at the end of the queue,' said the clerk, suddenly alert and filled with fury.

I grabbed the form he held and tore it in two. 'Ye know whit ye can dae wi' that,' I said.

On the way out I gave the guys on the bench a V sign to which they responded with loud catcalls and jeers. Outside I stood on the steps, marked in black paint with the words FUCK THIS BROO, bracing myself for the only option ahead of me, and that was to accept Duds Smith's offer.

I nearly ran all the way back to his caravan yard when I started to consider that there were many possibilities in driving a low-loader. For instance, I could be sent up to the northern coast. It was possible I might bump into Nancy. It's a small world and this is a small country. I could even make a point of looking her up, come to that, all spruced up, the owner of a caravan and earning a weekly wage. She could only be impressed and overjoyed to see me again. As I strode rapidly along the road I laughed aloud at the extravagance of my thoughts. A woman passing, wearing a headscarf and carrying a bag of messages, gave me a startled look.

'It's a fine day for a chinge, missus,' I said.

Her face softened as she said, 'Aye, it's no' bad at a', son. We canny complain.'